GUN MAN

GUN MAN

LOREN D. ESTLEMAN

DOUBLEDAY & COMPANY, INC.

GARDEN CITY, NEW YORK

1985

Library of Congress Cataloging in Publication Data

Estleman, Loren D.
Gun man.

I. Title.
PS3555.S84G8   1985   813'.54
ISBN 0-385-23067-2
Library of Congress Catalog Card Number: 85-10248
Copyright © 1985 by Loren D. Estleman

To Jory and Charlotte Sherman

GUN MAN

CHAPTER ONE

His pa he worked the dirt and dust
a-strainin in the sun;
But John he let the plow grow rust
and practiced with his gun.

He was born Eugene Morner in the later county of Blackhawk, Iowa, April 6, 1842, and when the newspapers learned of it thirty years later they made a lot of the surname and kept wanting to put a *u* in it.

His father was a tenant farmer who left a wife and two children in Scotland and married a Delaware girl before pushing west with Eugene four months in the womb. Morner used the last of the money he had borrowed from his new father-in-law to buy 160 acres at a tax auction and worked them for twelve years, sometimes helping out at the mill in Waterloo to support a family that would eventually include Eugene, his brothers Jerome and Matthew, and their sister Maureen.

His mother was Irish, the daughter of a former New York City alderman who by the time he was forty had made enough off the overage from the construction of an unnecessary bridge over the Hudson to retire to Delaware. A small, brown-haired woman with quick eyes and a chin that Eugene would remember as always shot past her toes, she had during a childhood at Tammany formed no illusions about the ways of men while learning a lifelong respect for the virtues of organization. It was she who kept the accounts on the farm and decided whether it was time to invest in a new plow or to retrench and make do with the old one. They did not grow rich, but they subsisted, and during the depression of 1848 the Morners were the only farming family in the community not on credit at the mercantile.

A week before Eugene's twelfth birthday, his father bent to replace a cracked leather hinge on the door to the stall of a mule named Dick and caught a sharp hoof in his right temple. He got up, dusted straw and manure off his trousers, picked up a three-legged milk stool, and shattered Dick's spine with a swing that reduced the stool to splinters. Then he went back into the house, sat down in his place at table, and died.

Eugene's mother had Dick's carcass dragged to a ravine and emptied the cash box to bury her husband and hire a Negro man to do the plowing and fixing. When that was arranged she called Eugene to the kitchen end of the little frame house with loft and looked at him for a long time from her seat at the table she used for a desk between meals, and where her husband had died. She saw a tawny-headed boy small for his years, but burned brown and thong-muscled from walking in front of his father's plow and bending to lift rocks and hurl them out of its path. His eyes were mud-colored but quick like hers and he had a man's jaw, long and square and already glinting with fine down.

"What's five and two?" she asked finally.

"Seven."

"And three and six."

He thought. "Nine."

"Spell horse."

He spelled it, reciting the word before and after, the way he'd been taught.

"You can write your name?"

He nodded. Her unmoving gaze made him fidget.

She sat back, and sunlight leaning in through the window inlaid fine silver in her thick dark hair. "Monday morning we're going to town, you and I."

"Monday's school."

"No, your schooling is finished. Monday you're going to ask Mr. Sharon for a job with his freighting company."

A Catherine wheel burst in the boy's chest, spraying pride all over. But he had inherited nothing from his mother if not the ability to dissemble his eagerness. "Well, why do I need you there, if I'm going to be the one doing the asking?"

She slapped him, hard enough to make his eyes smart and his nose run.

"Don't ask why," she said. "Don't ever ask why. You've just lost your father and you're not thinking right, so I'll tell you just this once, but don't do it again. If you get the job and I'm not there you'll receive a boy's wages, and it takes more than that to keep Henry working this place. This is free territory—we can't ask him to work for nothing."

"How will you being there make Mr. Sharon pay me a man's wages?"

"He will, don't worry. All you have to worry about is showing him you can do what you'll be hired for."

He never did know why Sharon gave in so early and agreed to pay grown wages for a boy's work, but in later years he thought about it often. George Sharon, despite his girlish surname, was a big man with long curling hair and a rectangular black beard rolled and steamed into horizontal waves like corrugated metal that reminded Eugene of the woodcut of Pharaoh in *The Young People's Book of Bible Stories*, and his chest and shoulders seemed contained only by a truce with his vest and dusty frock coat. One minute he was in his pine-smelling office protesting the bargain Eugene's mother proposed, and the next he was in the wagon yard showing the boy how to grease the axles so that the thick black stuff wound up where it was needed. Long after Sharon was laid to rest with a Mormon bullet in his brain and he himself no longer answered to Eugene Morner, he would think back and try to remember the words that were said in that office, but always without success. It was the only question he would ever again ask with a why in it.

At the end of his first day, grease under his nails and his muscles smarting from loading and unloading the same wagon with the same rocks, which Sharon had set for his first test in his determination to wrest a man's work out of him, Eugene was halted in mid-climb to his bed in the loft by his mother's call. She wanted to show him something.

He stood weaving in the curtained entrance to his parents' bedroom, literally asleep on his feet, while she drew from under a pillow a long bundle wrapped in cotton ticking. With no real respect for her late husband's wrapping she unwound the cloth and held out a long revolver with a smooth cylinder and a hard black rubber grip.

He took it carefully. He had handled it many times, alone in the house while his father was in the field and his mother was out pumping water and his brothers and sister were playing in the barn, but never with their knowledge. It weighed nearly three pounds and it was the most grown-up thing he had ever held.

"It's a Colt's Paterson," she told him. "Your father bought it direct from the New Jersey plant. He got it for Indians, but there aren't many out here and he kept it cleaned and loaded in case of intruders. I want to keep it here for that reason while you're away working. But it's your responsibility now. When you're rested I'll show you how to oil and load it the way your father showed me coming over."

Reluctantly he surrendered the weapon and she rebound it and returned it to its place. In bed he thought of it, its blue gloss and the cold of the metal even in a heated building, and thinking of it he fell asleep.

Whatever baby fat still clung to his frame burned off in his first month with Sharon & Co. Freighters. He greased axles, fetched water to cursing wheelers and laborers sweating to fill and empty the wagons, helped stretch canvas, carried messages, worked the bellows of the forge while the smith, a big Pole whose name Eugene could not pronounce, burned as black as old Henry, heated the iron ferrules for the wheels to an orange glow and then hammered them straight on the great flat hunk of obsidian he preferred to an anvil. The boy's muscles grew along with his vocabulary of oaths.

Midafternoon of a warm day in early May, between chores, he stretched out on his back in the wagon yard with an arm flung across his eyes to keep out the sun and dozed, only to waken when the cool of a shadow touched him. His sleep was light by nature and his senses were abnormally acute. He looked up at Sharon's bulk blacking out the sun. Beside him stood another man, much smaller, clad in a derby and a white linen duster whose hem scuffed the tops of his boots. His eyes were light-colored in the shadow of his narrow hat brim and he wore a beard that at first glance looked like a week's worth of stubble. Eugene scrambled to his feet.

"Gene, this is Ben Honey, one of my partners."

"Sir." Eugene moved only his head in greeting. In 1854 boys did not shake hands with men.

Honey's light eyes moved over him slowly. He was scarcely an inch taller than the boy and no more broad. "He is sort of hollow in the flanks," Honey observed.

"He's stronger than he looks. He can lift nearly as much as some of the men."

"I hope so. I don't want any boys dying on me."

"It's not that arduous a trip, surely."

"I cannot say. No one has ever made it, not with a train of freight. The Cheyennes will smell the booty and paint their faces and then we will have us some hell."

"Gene is my best boy," Sharon said.

"He is your only boy."

Eugene fidgeted. He had a fierce sense of self—his father had called it the devil in him—and didn't care to hear himself discussed in his own presence as if he were mule meat. But he kept silent. Finally Sharon said: "Gene, Mr. Honey is getting up a freight expedition into Indian country, although by the time you get there it will be Nebraska territory, if the Congress climbs off the pot. The cargo will include lumber and nails for the capital."

"Nebraska City, although Omaha is making its own push." Honey was speaking more to his partner than to Eugene. "The expedition is speculative."

"Wise too, I hope. Every free cent we have is tied up in it."

"Where else would they establish their capital, if not in the territory's namesake?"

"You forget, sir, I was reared in Albany." To Eugene: "You will function as an extra, which means just what it sounds like. Whenever something is to be done that is too meager or time-consuming for the scouts and drivers, it will fall to you. The work will be harder than what you are doing now, and the hours much longer. But you will see some new country."

"More of the same, only bigger. The boy will do. We leave Monday at first light." The man in the derby and duster shook Sharon's hand and left without once having addressed Eugene. The senior partner sensed the boy's resentment.

"Honey is a hard man but a good one, and dependable," he said. "He was commissioned in the war with Mexico. If there is trouble he will bring you through it." The expression behind the biblical beard softened. "You needn't go. You'll be a month away from your mother and work on the farm."

"My brothers can help Henry. And the extra money will come handy."

Sharon grunted. "No one said there was extra money in it."

"Sir, no one said there wasn't."

"You're your mother's child, boy. Go tell her now. Get the crying over early."

"She won't cry."

"No, I don't believe she will."

She didn't. Seated at the table, nursing Maureen—Eugene's sister was almost two and not yet weaned—she let him finish, then put down the girl and buttoned her blouse to the neck. "You'll need the rifle." She was referring to the flintlock her husband had used for squirrel, leaning next to the hearth. The boy had been shooting small game with it since his eleventh birthday.

"No, the revolver," he said. "There will be Indians and I'll need more than one shot."

"You talk as if you'd welcome the chance."

"Well, if it presents itself."

"I saw a man killed once, in the courthouse in New York City. Blood came out of his ears. If a man must kill another man he should at least be reluctant."

"A man, yes. An Indian—"

"You've never seen an Indian."

"I will out there, Mr. Honey said."

"Ben Honey is empty. His eyes are like bottle tops and the bottles have nothing in them."

"You *know* him?"

"You don't know men like Ben Honey. You say hello to them when they cross your path and keep walking."

"Mr. Sharon says he's dependable."

"So is the devil. You can depend on him to be wicked."

"I can't go?"

"Men without souls are necessary out there." She rose. "I'll get the revolver."

When the weapon changed hands, little Maureen's grave pretty eyes followed it. "Eugene bang," she said.

CHAPTER TWO

When still a boy he killed a man,
in years he was just twelve;
His gun flashed lightning in his hand
and put the man in Hell.

To a boy reared in a country without horizons, the word "big" meant no more than the word "snow" meant to an Eskimo. Eugene could distinguish a big horse from a small one, and Lord and his back knew the difference between a big rock and a stone fit for throwing, but he could never understand the transformation in his father's and his father's friends' faces when they employed the word, not until two weeks of constant movement with eight ox-drawn wagons and to-bacco-spittle-smelling bullwhackers brought no change either in the scenery or in the smoky blue line where earth met sky in the west. The world was round, all right, and it just kept rolling, so that a fellow could walk holes in his feet from first light to last and camp on the spot where he had camped a week before. The oxen lumbered along at three miles per day, or sprinted at four, and neither whip nor the fat green flies glittering around their rumps and nostrils could get another yard out of them. Walking alongside the train and staying available for whatever errand occurred to the driver whose eye he caught, he sometimes forgot himself and had to walk back or wait for the wagons to catch up. On these occasions the lead driver would squirt brown juice, only a little of which cleared his whiskers, and send the boy back with a message, or out to collect wood or buffalo chips for that night's fire, growling something about putting all that young piss and vinegar to use. The trips back or out were rare that didn't collect at least two or three more jobs from the other drivers he encountered. Beyond that few of the men spoke to him.

Ben Honey spent most of his time horseback with one or the other of the two scouts hired to ride ahead and hang an eye out for the Indians who sometimes wandered across the Missouri looking for game or plunder. Sometimes he camped with the scouts, but oftener he rode back nights to chuck with the drivers and wrap himself in a blanket under the star-pierced sky, or under a wagon when it rained. These times if he had something for Eugene to do he relayed the order through a driver. If he didn't look so right in the saddle, wearing a hard hat with a broad flat brim in place of his derby but otherwise dressed as when Eugene had first seen him, down to the duster and town boots, the boy might have thought him afraid of children, not an uncommon trait among men he had observed. But uncommon enough in men who rode with Indian scouts, or so he was comfortable believing.

One night, having helped the lead driver remove the yoke from his team, Eugene was called upon for a light. He took a match from the oilcloth he had taken to carrying, lit the lantern that swung from a rib of the wagon, and held it up while the driver examined the great shoulders of the ox he called Hector. The light glistened on the gout from a running sore where the yoke had rubbed. The driver, a German, said something guttural, then switched to English.

"Fistulated. Cut me a plug."

The boy carried the lantern to the back of the wagon, plucked a gold-foil package of brown mule from an open crate, and used his pocketknife to saw off a piece the length of his thumb. It was one of his jobs to supply the driver with a fresh plug mornings, but this was the first time it had been demanded at this hour. He put the package in his pocket along with the knife and brought the lantern and the hard lump to the front of the wagon. Honey was there.

"We espied a small band of bucks heading north this afternoon," he was saying. "The train will cross their path tomorrow if they don't change directions."

"War party?" The German took the plug from the boy and popped it into the hole in his beard.

"We did not get that close. Not, I think, this far east. They will be looking for handouts."

"How many?"

"Not more than eight or nine."

"They have no use for pine boards and tenpenny nails."

Honey looked down at his boots, his hatbrim hiding his face. "The last wagon contains whiskey for the saloons in Nebraska City."

The driver swore, in English this time.

"Only the driver knows of it," Honey went on, "and he is a teeto-taler. I did not want the word to get around."

The German chewed rapidly, making squishing noises in the last remaining section in his mouth where two rows of teeth met. Snarling to Eugene to hold the light steady, he expectorated into a leathern palm and smeared the glutinous stuff over the running sore in Hec-tor's hide. The ox flinched at the first touch and jerked its huge head sideways. Very soon, however, as the tobacco began drawing off the poison, the animal blew out its nostrils, a long grunting sigh of relief.

"We cannot give them whiskey," said the German, kneading the rude medicine deep into the wound. "The devils will play hell with whoever comes behind us."

"I know."

"I have a case of chew in the wagon."

"So has every other driver in the expedition. Indians don't use it."

"They can dry and shred it for smoking."

"That is too much work. Among us we may put together as much as a case of smoking tobacco, but there are eight wagons and your usual buck is fixated on elementary arithmetic."

"What else have we to trade?"

Honey's hat brim came up. His pale eyes reflected the lantern light. He said nothing.

"I have a revolver in the wagon," spoke up Eugene.

The German ignored him. "It is not worth a fight for what we will get on this cargo in Nebraska City. You know I was against this from the start. They can float all the building materials they need up the Missouri at half the cost."

"Not one boat in three makes it past the river pirates above Kansas City without paying tribute equal to three times the cargo's worth."

"You can bargain with Christians. A frustrated Indian will kill you and take everything."

"Well, I am not giving them whiskey."

Honey went off. The driver watched his back for a moment, then untied the kerchief from around his own neck and used it to complete the poultice, plastering it to the tobacco that now covered the raw spot. "I hope whoever comes behind us appreciates the gesture," he muttered.

Eugene fed the animals, ate something at the campfire, and rolled into his blanket on the opposite side of the wagon from the lead driver. For the first time on a journey that bored him into exhaustion he didn't sleep right away. The Colt's Paterson was a solid lump of reassurance against his ribs.

Not all of it was boring. There was in the train a driver everyone called Curly, eighteen years and six feet of muscle and hard fat under a shock of wild yellow hair and a drooling set of moustaches shadowing jowls more suited to a man much older, who had taken a dislike to Eugene from the first day. When his wagon threw a wheel he had ordered the boy to fix it, a two-man job at best and the sort of responsibility that normally fell to the driver. When Eugene took twice as long as customary at it, Curly called him a lazy suckling pig and scuffed his ribs roughly with the sole of a hobnail boot. Days later Eugene still felt the effects every time he drew a breath. The young driver seldom missed a chance to box the boy's ear as he walked past or grab a fistful of hair on the back of his neck and worry it painfully. Outweighed by a hundred pounds, Eugene said nothing and took no action other than to watch his back whenever Curly's nasal bray came within earshot. Because he had known fear, he knew that what he experienced on these occasions was not that. He reckoned that it was hate.

The morning after the exchange between Honey and the German driver, the boy awoke with a familiar smell in his nose that seemed much stronger than usual. Smelling it, he swam up through layers of sleep as thick as Hector's tobacco poultice and opened his eyes on the leaden light of false dawn. Looking down at his blanket, he saw it was smeared with something that glistened. The stink was overpowering. Revolted, he tore the blanket aside, and then he heard a braying laugh and looked up at Curly standing over him, wiping his palms on a double handful of last year's grass.

"You been walking behind them oxes too long, kid," he said. "You're commencing to smell like them."

Without thought Eugene clenched his fingers around the Colt's

butt. Just then the German inserted his broad back in front of him.
"Curly, see to your team."

The young driver ambled off, still laughing.

Turning to the boy, the German said:

"Scrub it around on the grass some. We will be at the Missouri day
after tomorrow and you can give it a proper washing then."

When the driver left, Eugene did as directed, the gun tucked in
the waistband of his corduroy trousers under his jacket. Neither of the
others had seen him grab for it in the poor light. He was shaking a
little, from the morning chill.

The sun was an hour down from noon when they saw the Indians.
Johnson, the elder of the two scouts, shaggy-haired and graying and
dressed disappointingly (for Eugene) in ordinary homespun with a
Hawken rifle slung from his saddle ring, had been riding with the
wagons all morning beside Ben Honey, who halted the train and
accompanied the frontiersman up the hill to where the naked riders
sat their paints. From where Eugene was standing by the lead wagon
he could see that their hair was plaited and that some of them wore
feathers, but of the great warbonnets he had expected there was no
sign. Their bows and lances and the curved stock of one very long rifle
stuck up behind their backs, thorny against the empty sky.

"Brown Bess, or I am damned." The German spat. "His grandfather must have traded it off some redcoat." He himself sat with a
Jaeger rifle across his knees. A casual glance back along the line of
wagons revealed a long barrel protruding from each.

"They're not painted," observed the boy, loosening his own
weapon.

"Sometimes they aren't. It would be like running up the skull and
crossbones too early."

For a long time they watched the riders. While Honey remained
unmoving astride his bay, his shaggy companion gestured broadly,
making quick jerking movements with his hands. The Indian who
seemed to be the spokesman for the party, tall-riding and holding a
lance with feathers trailing from the tip, interrupted often with ges-
tures of his own, these even more slashing and abrupt. When he
thumped his chest, Eugene swore he heard the noise. This went on
for several minutes. Then Honey turned in his saddle and raised his
right arm.

"That's us," said the German. "Get the chew and carry it on up."

Heart drumming, the boy lifted the open crate out of the bed and started up the grassy slope. It was a longer walk than it looked, and all the way he could feel the eyes of the drivers behind him and of the Indians and two white men in front of him. He was careful to come in from the side to avoid spooking the horses, and at last, obeying a gesture from Honey, he set down his burden in front of the Cheyenne spokesman's horse and backed away. This close he could smell the rancid grease on their bodies and see the utter lack of shine in their black eyes. Their faces were flat and gave up no more expression than a Chinaman's.

After a lengthy silence the spokesman's lance moved and another brave hopped down from his horse and reached into the crate and handed up one of the foil packages. The mounted Indian tore it open with his teeth and sniffed the contents. His face screwed up. He threw the package to the ground and said something in a tongue that reminded Eugene of his brother Jerome talking backwards, only much harsher.

"He says it's dogshit," Johnson told Honey, when the barrage had stopped. "He wants whiskey."

"Tell him we have no whiskey."

The scout moved his hand twice, too rapidly for Eugene to follow. Even so, the Indian was gesturing before he finished.

"He says he can smell it from here."

"Can he?" Honey's eyes never left the Indian's face.

"No, he's bluffing."

"Tell him we cannot give him what we do not have."

The response this time was longer and more complicated.

"He says if your tongue is true you won't mind one of his bucks having hisself a look-see."

"If an Indian comes within a hundred yards of one of those wagons he will find his fare paid to the happy hunting ground."

"You want me to tell him that?"

"I am not talking just to hear my own tongue flap."

Johnson relayed the message. The Indian spokesman stiffened. The hilltop got quiet, as if a heavy wind had suddenly stopped blowing. Silence shouted. Then the brave mounted next to the spokesman leaned over and whispered in his ear. Listening, he fixed his black eyes on Eugene, who felt a dark cave open inside his chest. The head Indian nodded, then fluttered his hand in front of the scout and pointed to Eugene.

"He's asking is the boy yours."

Honey started. "Why?"

"He says if you have no whiskey he will take the boy and raise him up Cheyenne."

Eugene reached quickly under his jacket. Instantly he was staring at the pointed ends of what appeared to be a dozen lances.

"Lay up, kid," Johnson said. "Take your hand out slow and empty."

Reluctantly he obeyed.

A ripple of amused sounds swept through the Cheyenne party; it could not quite be called laughter. Their leader's mouth turned up and he swiveled his head to beam on the brave on either side of him. The lances came down. He spoke to Johnson, accentuating the grunts with his free hand.

"He'll take the boy and you can keep the baccy," translated the scout.

"Tell him free white men are not in the habit of bartering with boys. Take the tobacco and go in peace."

Another long pause followed this information, as charged as the first. Johnson worked a wad of chew, his eyes darting. Finally the spokesman barked and the Indian who had dismounted reached again into the crate and tossed packages one by one to the others, who caught them with a show of reflexes Eugene found remarkable. The remaining items were proffered to the leader, who put them away in the war bag on his rude hide saddle. Then as one, and on no signal that Eugene saw or heard, the entire party of nine wheeled their horses and struck off west at a walk.

"They'll come painted next time," said Johnson, watching.

"We shall be waiting when they do." Honey turned his bay and started back down the hill toward the wagons.

By midafternoon the story of the Cheyennes' offer had spread to the last driver, and when they made camp that night Eugene found himself pummeled and his head rubbed by hands thick with callus. "Ourght to think 'er over, lad," said one. "Get yourself one of them squaws to do the work for you, sit and get waited on like some oriental pottin' take."

All of this sudden attention on top of weeks of being ignored embarrassed him, and he was glad enough when the joshing died down and it was time to make his bed. He was reaching inside the wagon for the desecrated blanket when a hand bulled under his jacket and the gun was torn out of his pants.

"This here's too much iron for a sprout like you," brayed Curly. "I'll just hang onto it till Nebrasky."

Whirling, Eugene glared at the fat driver fingering his weapon. "Give it back!"

"Well, supposing you take it." Curly shoved the barrel under his belt in front, where his belly bulged around the butt like bread dough. Smirking, he tucked his thumbs inside the belt on either side of it.

The boy sprang, butting his head hard into the arch of Curly's ribcage. Rewarded with a loud *woof*, he clawed for the revolver. The driver grabbed for it just as the barrel came free, pulling Eugene's finger tight on the trigger. The roar was swallowed in the flesh around Curly's middle.

The driver took two steps backward, eyes and mouth working. He looked down at the dark stuff blossoming between the fingers clasped on his belly and sat down on the ground.

Ben Honey was first on the scene. Hatless, his dark hair spidery thin in front, he glanced from the wounded driver to the boy standing with the revolver in two hands in the lantern light. Then he addressed Eugene for the first time.

"Commencing sort of young, aren't you, boy?"

CHAPTER THREE

He took the outlaw trail then,
half-growed as he were;
A schoolboy at the age of ten,
at twelve a runnin cur.

Within minutes, Eugene and the man gasping on the ground were the center of a crowd of jabbering drivers, through which Johnson forced his way. He had his suspenders up over white flannels gone gray from washing and not washing and he smelled sharply of whiskey. He took in the scene at a glance and looked at Honey. "Gutshot?"

"Yes."

He stood over the driver. "You're a gone beaver, Curly. You want to go back home, or can we put you in the ground here?"

"I want a doctor." Pink bubbles flecked his lips.

"You wouldn't make it halfway. Boy, who's your kin?"

It took Eugene a second to realize he'd been addressed. "My name's Morner."

"Well, you best take the borry of a horse and get back to them. This here's Devil Cook's cousin."

Honey closed a hand around the Colt's cylinder. After a moment's resistance Eugene let him take it. Devil Cook was the train's other scout, a quiet lean dark man in his late twenties with old knife scars on both cheeks. The boy had seen him only twice since the expedition started and had never heard him utter a word.

"He would take vengeance on a boy?" Honey asked.

"He ain't called Devil on account of he likes chocolate cake. When he gets back and finds Curly cold as a lizard he'll want him some blood."

Curly said, "I want a doctor."

"Do what you can for him," Honey told Johnson. "Back to your bedrolls, the rest of you. Come with me, boy."

As the drivers dispersed, the German looking back at him thoughtfully, Eugene accompanied Ben Honey into the shadows beyond the lantern light. They walked for several minutes, and then a long, shuddering snort told the boy they were near the horses. Honey stopped.

"Here. You may have need for it."

Moonlight striped the barrel of the Colt's Paterson. Eugene took it.

"Do you ride, boy?"

"Yes."

"You know my bay," the man said. "He is skittish with a strange rider so I want you to stay here and make friends while I fetch my saddle and provisions. I expect he can carry you and one week's worth. That should see you to Springfield even if you stick to the back roads, which I strongly advise. Keep the North Star at your back nights and the sun on your left mornings. When you get there ask for Sam Woodlawn. Remember the name. Tell him I sent you and he will have work for you."

"I can't go home?"

"Home is where boys run. Cook will go there first, and then he will try west. He will not think to look for a boy in a hellhole like Springfield."

Eugene stared at Honey, or rather at those parts of his face that picked up the moon. The light eyes were invisible. He did not ask the question his mother had warned him against. But the man heard it anyway.

"George Sharon promised your mother I would look to your best interest. When a man you would give your word to gives it for you, you are as bound as if you gave it yourself. He will tell her you are in sound hands. In six months, a year perhaps, you can go back. A man's anger burns short out here and I cannot imagine anyone shedding bitter tears over the like of Curly longer than that. The bay's name is Byron, like the poet's. He will get you where you are headed. Look to him, mind; he is your wages for this expedition."

The bay sidled from him, but it was picketed, and Eugene caught it and stroked its neck, making lowing noises and giving it time to grow used to him, the way he had seen his father behave with Dick when the mule was new to the farm; but that image was bad luck and he wiped it out as soon as it came to him. In camp, Curly had begun to whimper, the sound eerily inhuman on the night air.

Inside the circle of wagons, the German driver watched Ben Honey shoving tins of food and a kerchief bulging with hardtack into his scuffed saddlebags. The others had rolled the wounded man into a blanket and he lay on his side with his knees drawn into his chest, making cat sounds. Across the circle, an enterprising bullwhacker with a railroad watch made his way among his fellow drivers, peddling chances on the ,hour of Curly's death.

"Devil Cook is wild, but not wild enough to touch a boy or a man under your protection," the German said. "There is no need to send the boy fleeing."

"When you kill a man you have to be prepared to defend yourself or run." Honey hefted the loaded pouches, frowned, and removed two tins from each. Then he secured the flaps and slung them over his shoulder.

"The shooting was an accident."

"I am not so certain."

The German followed him to where he had left his saddle with his bedding. "A killer at twelve?"

"I was fourteen."

"Times then were different."

"People were not." Honey hoisted the saddle—like himself, a Mexican War veteran—and faced the driver briefly before leaving the light. "Has it not occurred to you that in order to go off, that gun had first to have been cocked and primed?"

It was a chill night, the saddle stiff and slippery for the first several miles until the heat of horse and boy limbered it. Eugene put the polestar at his back and let the bay pick its way carefully, avoiding chuckholes. Alone as he had ever been, he found himself thinking about home things: the cold of his first contact with the sheets on his bed in the loft on a winter evening, until his own body heat filled the pocket where he lay; his mother's baking spreading its cuddlesome smell throughout the house mornings; the clean, crisp *chomp* of a potato fork introducing itself to the turned earth in the north forty.

His sister would be asleep by now, Jerome and Matthew too, if they weren't wrestling with each other, his mother opening the stove to lay in a piece of hickory before shutting it down for the night. Eugene felt and smelled and heard these things. And loneliness wrapped itself around him like a shroud of ice under his clothes, and he cried.

But as the horse carried him onward, each step tautening the cord that bound him to the expedition, and to the cords that bound it to home, until it snapped, he knew a thrill of new things to do and see, and by the time the first pale glow lifted the sky from the earth to let the dawn through, he felt his senses opening like hundreds of tiny eyes. The air was sharp and clean and the bay's shoes rang like church bells on the hard earth. Colors he had never seen were waiting to show themselves to him when the light was right. He felt fresh-born.

At the time he confused the feeling with freedom, but in later years he would come to know it as the inevitable aftermath of having killed.

By late morning he was dozing in the saddle. He turned off the road into a grove of trees and tied up Byron, letting him graze while he fixed himself a bed of winterkilled grass. Ben Honey had given him his blanket to take the place of his own befouled one but he didn't use it. The sun was warm. He slept quickly, and awoke in the late daylight to eat a hard biscuit and cover some more ground before sundown.

In the beginning much of his journey took him through open country, hundreds of miles of flat grassland wheeling out from his own center with trees sprouting in cowering clumps like hairs from a witch's wart, hawks drawing slow loops on the pale blackboard of the sky. When he saw smoke on the horizon he altered his course not to intersect it. He imagined the news of his act sparking ahead of him like Mr. Morse's code, his name and description going up on trees and barns and men with cigars and derbies shoving things of his at the snouts of loose-skinned dogs and the dogs galloping down his trail, kiyoodling like Mr. Skinner's wolfhound the night it grounded a skunk under its master's house and sent Mr. Skinner to the hotel in Waterloo for a week. The fugitive life opened his pores and made his skin crackle.

Farther south, the scattered smoke columns mingled, and he knew he was nearing the Missouri line, where he would have to watch himself in earnest, for he had heard stories of bandits in the hills and of people who called themselves slavers and abolitionists, regardless of whether they had ever kept or freed a slave, but who were always fighting, and an innocent wanderer could get himself caught in the middle. Thought of it made his blood glow. He unseated the Colt's, ran a willow twig through the barrel to clear away the worst of the powder he had spent on Curly, and fed shot and ball and cotton wadding into the vacant chamber from the supply in his pocket. The rough who tried to take advantage of a companionless boy would find himself face to face with a blooded killer.

Nights he opened whatever tins came first to his hands and scooped the contents into his mouth with his pocket knife, washing them down with water from Ben Honey's canteen. He had matches but did not make a fire, fearful of what the smoke might attract. Once, while he was putting away the knife, his hand came in contact with something in his pocket and he drew out the package of chewing tobacco he had put there the night the German driver had nursed the ox Hector. He cut himself a plug and tried it, but he swallowed some of the sweet thick juice and gagged and spent much of the next hour wasting his supper into a bush. He put the remainder back in his pocket and never again used tobacco in any form the rest of his life. He would come to equate the habit with a fatal nervousness and charge at least three wooden crosses to its advantage to him and disadvantage to others.

One day short of the Missouri border, Byron stepped on a gopher mound that collapsed under his right forefoot, twisting it and tearing tendons. Eugene was thrown, but landed on his feet, and after examining the damage, knew that from then on he was afoot.

For the first time since leaving the train he felt real fear. In the back of his mind he had allowed to lurk the notion that Devil Cook was behind him, wilier than Ben Honey's assessment, knowing Honey's own mind and the kind of advice he would give and that his cousin's killer would be on the road to Missouri. While on horseback he had been able to dismiss it as the sort of worry that comes in the night and fades like frost on glass with sunrise. On foot it was as solid and undeniable as ground ice in January. With his heart slamming his ribs he started leading Byron, the bay putting weight on the injured leg gingerly, squealing, and drawing it up, hobbling on the others. In this manner they made a mile in the time it normally took to cover five.

It was because the boy was so preoccupied with this situation that he failed to avoid meeting the first human being he had seen in three days.

The splutter of a strange horse alerted him. He drew back behind the cluster of trees he was coming around, too late to avoid being seen by his new acquaintance. This individual sat a blue roan on the other side of a brown creek with rushes on the banks, naked but for a leather breechclout and low summer moccasins. He was a young brave not more than two years older than Eugene, wearing the plaited hair and longbow the boy had come to associate with the Cheyennes. Only the roan's front hoofs were in the water. The youth had been about to cross when he'd spotted Eugene and drawn rein.

For at least a minute they watched each other without moving, Eugene through a screen of leaves, the young Cheyenne exposed in bright sunlight. Then, with a speed and grace that the white boy admired even as panic soared within him, the youth unslung his bow, skinned an arrow out of the quiver across his shoulders, and notched it. He was drawing when Eugene stepped out into the open, hands raised.

The Indian paused. The arrow was drawn its full length, his thumb at the corner of his jaw. His black eyes reflected no light and he appeared not to breathe. Even his mount was still.

Eugene's mind was working as fast as only a boy's can in the confidence of his own immortality. Indians loved tribute; that much he had learned in his brief experience with them. What to trade for his life? And in the asking he knew the answer.

Moving more slowly than he had ever moved, he lowered his right hand. The bicep in the Cheyenne's cocked right arm twitched. Eugene hesitated, then resumed. The hand descended to his jacket pocket, paused inside, and came out grasping the gold-wrapped plug of tobacco. He raised it just as slowly, holding it out, letting the foil catch the light. He suspected that Indians were attracted to bright things.

Long after he had lost all feeling in the arm, he stood holding the item (he reflected later, amusedly) like a cigar-store chief. He feared that it would drop suddenly, startling the youth into firing the arrow.

When he was sure that it was about to do just that, the Indian moved.

The bow came down. The string remained taut, the weapon ready to raise and fire. He posed like that, and Eugene realized the next move was his. He took a step forward, another, and then he was walking—if not naturally, at least he was not skulking. When he reached the creek he stopped again. The bow came down the rest of the way and the youth started across.

The roan tossed its dished head, grateful to be moving. Its fetlocks must have grown stiff in the icy current, because it stumbled a little starting, but Eugene could tell it was a good animal, if a little slat-sided from grass feeding. Its muscles moved like white water under its coat. The boy stepped back to allow horse and rider to mount the bank, and when the Cheyenne reached down to take the tobacco he dropped it and drew the revolver from under his jacket and shot him twice high on his naked chest.

Two blue spots appeared over the youth's left nipple and quickly turned red. There was no surprise on his face, only sudden knowing, and in the black eyes a flatness that was more flat than the flatness that had preceded it. The bow dropped. He reached for it out of reflex and the rest of his body followed. He struck the ground on his shoulder and rolled down the bank into the creek. The arm with which he had been reaching for the bow hung up on the reeds for a moment, but the rest of him was in the water and he slid away and floated. The current pushed at him and tried to turn him around.

The roan reared, but Eugene was ready and caught it by its hair bridle. He leaned his weight away from the hooking hoofs and made soothing noises until it stopped whistling and its forefeet came down. Its eyes rolled over white. The boy stroked its neck.

Sibilating softly through his teeth, feeling the great muscles roll beneath his palm, Eugene watched the breechclouted figure moving slowly downstream. He had heard stories about soldiers who had come back from the Mexican War with notches on their guns representing the Mexicans they had killed. He would never do such a thing with a fine gun like the Colt's Paterson. But if he did, he would now have two.

CHAPTER FOUR

Hares they run with other hares,
and wolves run with their like;
Killers hunt in packs and pairs—
in pairs and packs they strike.

The Cheyenne youth had ridden bareback, with only a bridle made from horsehair braided tough as new hemp. But an old brand on its hindquarters told the boy the horse had been broken to someone's saddle before the Indian or one of his people had either stolen it or (more likely) shot its owner off its back. Whenever he told the story later he would say he saw the brand right off and killed the brave in a fair fight out of outrage for his race. Along the way, too, the warrior's true age would be lost as cumbersome to the narrative.

However, guessing that it had been a long time since the roan had worn leather, he didn't try to saddle it, but tethered it to a ground root and left it there while he led Byron down the road and got out his revolver to kill again. This was much harder than disposing of either Curly or the Indian. Despite what had happened to his father, Eugene loved animals, and the unknowing trust in the lame bay's eye was almost too much for him as he cocked the hammer and fitted a fresh cap to the nipple and snugged the muzzle up behind the ridge of bone in back of the animal's right ear. He patted its neck and put a ball in its brain.

Afterward he stuffed his pockets with tins from the saddlebags, covered the carcass with grass and last year's dead leaves, and filled the canteen from the creek. The body was well on its way to Kansas by now if it hadn't hung up again in the rushes. Mounting the roan was difficult without a stirrup, doubly so after its master's death and the third report, whose echo had just finished snarling in the distance, and he took one spill when he had a knee over the animal's back and it fiddlefooted sideways, but after a few more false starts he got both fists in the coarse mane and a leg over the other side. When the roan tried to buck he turned it around in circles until it hung its head, waiting for the dizziness to pass. Eugene used his knees and the beast went several steps forward before realizing it had surrendered to a new rider. The boy had taken his training aboard a killer mule.

He had never crossed a border of any kind. He assumed there would be a sign, guards, some solid indication that he had passed into alien country. Later he reckoned he was twelve miles over the line before awakening to the knowledge that he had left Iowa. By then the geography had begun subtly to change, going from treeless plain to hills like groundswells, as if an enormous plow had raked the land, leaving furrows in which trees grew as thick as pepper plants and covered the slopes with deep green. These woods were rich in game. Birds skipped through the branches and once he saw sunlight bronze the antlers of a great elk before it turned quick as thought and crashed off through the brush. Rabbits were so plentiful, thudding away from the roan's approach, that when one exploded out almost underneath a hoof the horse hardly shied. For the first time the boy regretted not having taken his father's rifle when his mother offered it. He would never be as good at running shots with a hand weapon as he was with a long gun, and he craved meat.

The hills gentled into farm country, the rude trail broadening into a proper road pounded hard as brick by horses and wagons. He passed a wagon piled high with firewood going the other way, whose driver, bearded and weathered but not thirty, glared at him the way Eugene and his schoolmates had glared at children new to class. He remembered to touch his hat; not to would have been even more suspicious. For a moment as they drew abreast, the man appeared to be fighting whatever civil instincts he had, but eventually he lost and nodded gruffly just as they passed. Eugene wrestled the urge to turn and glance back over his shoulder. He knew he would only find the man doing the same, as if he didn't see a twelve-year-old boy riding with a Cheyenne bridle every day.

He saw more people—a boy on foot carrying a fishing pole, a farmer astride a mule using a stick to steer an old milk cow with a cataracted eye—and once a fat woman in a bonnet seated in a buggy next to a man in a celluloid collar bade him good afternoon. After this exchange he took a turning and found a road more winding and less traveled. By nightfall the whole community would know about the strange boy on the Indian horse.

For that reason he rode well past dark, putting distance between himself and the gossip. If Devil Cook was behind him (and with night that fear was back), he was leaving a trail as broad as a prairie fire for the avenger to follow. That night he slept in a ditch beside the road with a fresh primer cap under the revolver's hammer.

He awoke before dawn to the click of a steel shoe on a loose pebble in the road. The Colt's came out before the thought came in, the hammer back. He was getting that quick with it.

"Mister," drawled a man's voice from shadow, "I got me a thirty-six Navy pointed right about where I figure your bellybutton ought to be, but I don't much care if I'm three-four inches off. You should, though."

Eugene could see nothing in the chill darkness. The voice itself seemed to have come down from the sky. He sat with the heavy gun in both hands, the tethered roan snorting behind him, and stared up at the road until something darker than the night finally appeared to be seeping out of it, a high black bulk, a man on a horse looking down on him from twelve feet up.

"Mister, I want to hear that pistol clunk when it hits the road."

The voice was no more lively than before, but there was iron in it, and the boy knew without having to see that the Navy revolver alluded to was not an invention. He flicked the tiny copper cap off the Paterson with a thumb and rolled the hammer down and took a practice swing and then flipped the gun up out of the ditch, wincing when it clattered to the packed earth.

A long silence followed. Then clothing rustled, and a match cracked and flared startling white and burned down to a yellow nimbus. He blinked in the glare, sulphur fumes scraping his nostrils. He saw the highlights of a face that was mostly bone, cheeks without whiskers, two eye glints in hat-shadow. At least he wasn't wearing Devil Cook's scars. The vapor of his mount's breath squirmed in the flickering oval of light. The boy heard a surprised grunt. The match was blown out.

"Well, hell, you're fresh from the tit. I figured I catched me a real road agent. I throwed back bigger fish than you when I was hungry."

The man's accent was new, but American. Eugene had heard something like it the summer a peddler came through Waterloo. He had said he was from Virginia, but Eugene had overheard a neighbor telling his father he guessed he knew Arkansas trash when he saw it.

"Who's your people, boy?"

Eugene said nothing.

"Boy, you don't use that tongue I'm going to cut it off and salt it and fry it in bacon drippin's and eat it with my breakfast grind. I'm partial to tongue."

"I don't have any people."

"Well now. I guess I got to make do with jerk venison. You headed anywhere, or just taking up good ditch space?"

"Spring—" he started to say, and changed it. "St. Louis."

"Ask quick and the truth comes out first. What's in Springfield?"

He hesitated. "A job."

"Job." Another match blazed. As the man lit a cheroot, the light crawling over a hawk nose and dark-ringed eyes of no particular color, metal gleamed at his waist. The Navy was indeed real. He blew out the flame and broke the match audibly. "Who with?"

Eugene never discovered why he could not lie in this man's presence. He seemed not only to see in the dark, but to scour the skulls of man and boy and (as he often thought, later) to come out a little sadder than he had been going in.

"Sam Woodlawn," said Eugene.

"I know Sam Woodlawn. He hiring?"

"I was told he is."

The man smoked. The cheroot never left his lips, but the boy could tell when he was inhaling, because the orange tip glowed fiercely then, spreading light over his high narrow features. But for the eyes, muddy like his own, the face was disturbingly familiar. Indian.

"What do they call you when they don't call you boy, boy?" he asked then.

He was ready for that one, and answered without hesitation, determined to get out one lie. "John Miller."

The stranger tried it. "I don't reckon it much matters if what you call a dog or a man is right so long as he answers to it. Well, John

Miller, I'm Isham Eagle, and I can use the company to Springfield. You got to change your own drawers, though. I ain't hiring on as wet-nurse this trip."

"Eagle, that's an Indian name." Eugene stood. It was cold and damp in the ditch. His blanket was almost soaked through.

"My Cherokee maw would be surprised to hear it wasn't. She give it to me because of my nose and because my paw didn't get around to telling her his. Maybe you don't ride with breeds."

"I never did. I'm not fixing to ever."

"Then we'll be here a spell, because I ain't giving you my back and you ain't going ahead to wait for me down the road. A tree limb's good as a gun when nobody's looking."

He flicked a finger at the end of his cheroot, showering sparks that made the Navy in his belt gleam briefly.

Eugene wrung out his blanket. "I'll get my horse."

"Come fetch your hogleg first. Iron rusts quick down here."

The road wound through forest, and when the sun broke over the hills the riders were rinsed in leafy green light. Eagle was long-waisted but short in the legs—the boy noted that he wore his stirrups as high as he did himself, when he had them—and while the man's rough wool coat fell short in the sleeves, his trouser legs, turned up twice, still managed his instep. His hat brim was broad and bent down in front, the crown stained, and besides the revolver under his belt he carried a big Walker Colt in a saddle scabbard and a revolving rifle of the same make rolled up in a blanket behind the cantle.

The man himself might have been eighteen—but not Curly eighteen—or forty—but not George Sharon forty. His complexion was coarse but unlined and the hair that fell straight to his collar was blue-black. His face was as hairless as a boy's. He rode well, letting one arm hang.

"What kind of horse is that?" Eugene asked. It was a big gelding with a curved neck and spotted all over like a Dalmatian.

"Appaloosa."

"He sure is a beauty."

"After you get the looking done he is not much. Aps are contrary. All of them bloodlines get together in their brains and curdle them."

"They're that bad I'm surprised you ride one."

"He's what the man I took him from was riding."

They continued in silence for another mile. The hill country was starting again and they didn't push the horses, stopping at the top of each rise to let them blow.

"I don't reckon you got any fresh coffee in them pockets of yours," said Eagle during one of these pauses. "I'm down to last week's grounds."

"No coffee. I got victuals."

"Meat?"

"Sardines."

"Me too. I'm sweating oil now. Man needs fresh meat, he's going to ride all the way to Springfield."

"All I have is a pistol. If I had a rifle like you I'd eat rabbit."

"Colonel Colt's rifle is no better than an Appaloosa. When one chamber goes off, all the others fire too, like birds leaving a telegraph wire. A pistol is good enough for game."

"I wish you'd show me how."

Eagle made no reply, and Eugene thought he'd won his point and the half-breed was too stubborn to acknowledge it. A hundred yards farther on, a rabbit burst from the underbrush at the side of the road, wheeled at midpoint, and took off straight up the middle with its cottontail showing. Eagle drew the Navy with a long graceful movement of his right arm and fired. The hare heeled over, churning up dust, kicked once, and was still.

"Lord Jesus!" said the boy.

"Isham Eagle," corrected Eagle. "But I can see where the resemblance could fool a body."

They turned off the road and dismounted. While Eugene gathered firewood, Eagle skinned and cleaned the rabbit with the aid of a bowie knife and together they made a spit and took turns revolving it over the fire. They discovered they both preferred their meat charred outside. It was juicy and sweet and not too tough.

"Last of the season," said the man, with his mouth full. "One more week and they commence to take on worms."

Eugene was watching him over a dripping leg. "What do you do?"

"This and that. I get along."

"Well, where are you from?"

"Here and there. Eat your rabbit. It gets cold you'll be scraping tallow off the roof of your cake-hole all night."

"Can you teach me to shoot like that?"

"I'd consider it. If you'd tell me how is it a striplin' kid comes to sit a mount with a Cheyenne rig."

Eugene grinned, grease on his chin. "He's what the Cheyenne I took him from was riding."

Eagle's slow, answering grin was curiously downturned, with a black iron tooth in it.

CHAPTER FIVE

Springfield brewed a bitter stew
of slavers, roughs, and whores;
'Twas there that Killer Miller flew
in eighteen fifty-four.

In a later year, when dime novels were more common on the frontier than black Bibles, John Miller (for by then he had long since ceased to lift his eyes when his right name was called) would surprise many a tenderfoot who asked when he said that Isham Eagle was not fast with a gun. If in the right mood he would elaborate, explaining that others who were considered fast had been lying under dirt a long time, put there by men who were not. It was he who taught Eugene to take his time and be sure his gun had stopped moving before he pressed the trigger, and to wait for the smoke to clear before putting away his weapon, in case the first ball had not done its job. If this kind of advice seemed to have little to do with shooting rabbits, Eagle never embroidered on it, and Eugene never asked. In this manner they shot away most of a morning until Eugene grew low on primer caps and Eagle suspected someone might come to investigate the reports. They rode on, leaving behind two dead squirrels and enough blasted tree limbs to start a fire with wet green wood.

That afternoon they reached the Missouri River—broad and swift and brown as old skin. Eagle said he knew a place to cross and they followed the twisting bank east until they came to a clearing where a shack had been built of split logs with a smokehole in its slanted roof. There, a free mulatto with a glass eye, who seemed to know Eagle by sight if not by name, took a nickel from each of them and floated them and their horses across on a raft that was a better construction overall than the shack. All the way he regaled them with stories of how ferrymen from Independence came through a couple of times a week and held him at gunpoint while companions cut the cable he had strung across the river to guide the raft against the current. By noon of the next day he had the cable up again and spliced and was back in business until the next visit.

"Some night they'll sink the raft," Eagle suggested. "Or worse."

"Hell, no." Grunting, the mulatto worked the wooden lever that pulled the raft along the cable. " 'Thout me them boys got nothing to look forrard to 'cept pulling the ferry acrost in Independence. I is their Saturday night in Kansas City."

They thanked him for the ride and the story and led their horses off onto the rude quay built on the south bank. The mulatto pulled his way back across, singing "The True Lover's Lament." Two weeks later his body was found floating two miles downriver, shot full of holes.

Morning of their fourth day together found Eugene and Eagle in Springfield. Its size and traffic alarmed the boy, who had thought Waterloo as big as a place could grow. There were more proper frame buildings than log, and the main street was laid out straight and broad enough to turn a wagon and team around in, although a thing like that could not be attempted without causing a terrible accident; the street was that full of wagons and buggies and men straddling mules and big horses thick in the shanks. "Farmers," was Eagle's only comment, until he steered them to a rail in front of a long building with OZARK GENERAL MERCHANDISE painted inexpertly across the front. "Samuel T. Woodlawn, Prop."

Dismounting to tie up, Eugene felt his heart sink into his boots. He had left home in search of adventure and come all this way and killed two men to stack grainsacks in a general store.

They entered the establishment. It smelled of feed, an odor that Eugene realized in that moment he detested. Unopened crates and fat burlap sacks and tangles of harness left two narrow walkways open in front of displays of dress material and corncob pipes and a counter behind which a man as short as he, but twice as wide in the shoulders, stood working neat's-foot oil into a cracked leather halter. A fierce gray beard started at his eyes and grew straight down almost to his belt, with a twisted nose the color of iron bending over the thatch. Under calico sleeves his upper arms bulged like grapefruits as he kneaded the leather. When he turned his head their way, Eugene shuddered. The top of his right ear was gone and a purple welt as thick as a man's thumb angled up from it across his temple and into his hairline, eradicating half his right eyebrow. It seemed to glow red as he recognized Eagle.

"I told you what I had in mind for you iffen you ever poked your beak in here again, breed," he said. His voice was deep and rough, as if he were clearing his throat.

"Stand easy, Sam. I just got introducing to do and then I'm smoke."

A pair of terrible eyes regarded Eugene.

"He another one of your bastards, or you taken to liking little boys now?"

Eagle put a hand on Eugene's shoulder. "This here is John Miller. We met on the road. He says you're hiring."

"I ain't," Woodlawn said. "And iffen I was I wouldn't hire any-one'd ride with your like."

Eugene said, "Ben Honey said you'd have work for me."

The broad man worked leather in silence for a moment. Then: "Who'd you kill, boy?"

Startled, Eugene didn't answer.

"Last man Ben Honey sent me kilt him a state senator in Illinois. You kill anybody higher'n that?"

The boy shook his head.

"Because iffen you did, it means U.S. marshals coming, and where law goes people follow, and we got too damn many people out here now."

"I killed an Indian," Eugene said truthfully.

The hands worked. "Some digger, like as not. You'd about make breakfast for any real innun."

Eagle said, "He's riding a horse with a Cheyenne bridle."

"Hell you say." For the first time since they had entered, Wood-lawn's hands stopped working. He studied Eugene.

"Weren't it a Cheyenne tried to take your hair?" prodded the half-breed.

"Northern."

"Northern, Southern, they all smell the same to a Creek."

"Thought your maw was Cherokee."

"My paw weren't."

"A Irish drummer from Rhode Island, most like." Woodlawn resumed limbering the halter. "I got no need for innun killers today. Try the U.S. Army."

The boy spoke. "Ben Honey told me when a man you'd give your word to gives it for you, it's the same as you giving it yourself."

Oil squished in the cracks in the leather. The broad man's scowl deepened. "You come from Honey, all right. Be like him to put that bee on a friend he ain't seed in two year." He laid the halter aside and wiped his big hands on an apron made from a flour sack. "You handle a team?"

"Yes," Eugene lied.

"Uh-huh. It gets away from you, you better hope you fall out and land on your head, on account of iffen it does and you don't, I will. They's a wagonload of tools and provisions out back waiting on delivery down on the White River. I was fixing to take it myself, but seeing as you're here I can stay and pass the time with all these here fine folks in Springfield. Drop off your gear and I'll have her ready when you get back."

"I don't have any money for a place to stay."

"Well, ain't that sorrowful. Does this here look like Ma's Boardinghouse to you?"

"Come on, kid," said Eagle. "I got room, you don't mind sleeping on the floor."

Sam Woodlawn's whiskers moved, and Eugene guessed he was grinning in them, a diabolical sight. "Breed, you ain't got the floor to borry out. That young Widder Ashford's went and got herself a new beau."

"He got a name?" The half-breed's tone was dead.

"That Pete Dexter, Charlie Dexter's boy from up on the Osage. They's some tight, Pete and the widder."

"Well now," said Eagle, "I reckon she admires wearing black."

"Yeah." The beard was grave now. "Reckon she does."

Outside, the pair untied their mounts and led them down the street. "What'd you do to get him so mad at you?" Eugene asked.

"Woodlawn? Oh, he was one of the last of them to come down from the mountains after the beaver played out. That kind will trade with Indians and lay with their squaws but they only like them when they got need for them. Plus he thinks I sold a buckboard and team out from under him when I had that job he just give you."

"Did you?"

"White man's got no business trusting an Indian halfway, and less trusting half an Indian the rest of the way. I'm just a critter fulfilling his destiny. This here's the place."

They had stopped before what was for Springfield a truly fine house, and the sort of place Eugene always imagined when his father had told him, amid much profanity, of the manor house of the absentee English landlord on whose farm he had labored before leaving Scotland. It was two stories of whitewashed board with ornate designs painted on the lower window panes and a bed of flowers between the wall and the strip of grass in front. Behind it and to the left stood a carriage house of the same general design, but one-storied and windowless. It was this building that Eagle approached after handing his reins to Eugene and instructing him to wait. He opened one of the big front doors and went inside without knocking.

There was a long silence, and then something crashed inside. A thud. Another. One of the doors buckled outward once, loosing a thin shower of dust from a crack. A second crash. Another silence followed, longer than the first. Then the door opened and Eagle strode out, as casually as he had gone in. He came past Eugene and jerked loose the tie securing his bedroll with the rifle in it and shouldered it and turned back toward the carriage house.

Just then a woman opened the door of the main house from inside and came out on the porch. She had on a gray dress buttoned to the throat; its hem brushed her shoe tops. There were threads of gray in her reddish hair, which she wore pinned up. Eugene guessed she was his mother's age. Her cheekbones were high, the fine skin slightly flushed under a light application of powder, and she was looking down at Eagle with gray eyes as large as the mother-of-pearl buttons on the fox coat Eugene's mother had brought with her from Delaware. She was tall and stately—someone might have said hefty, but that someone wouldn't have been in love, as Eugene in that moment judged himself to be.

"Isham, what are you doing?"

"Moving back in." He stood watching her with the bedroll on his shoulder and his revolving rifle in his other hand.

"You may find it crowded."

At that moment a big man in his twenties, blond and baby-fat-looking in worn overalls, came out the open door of the carriage house carrying a carpetbag and heading for the street. As he drew near, Eugene saw the purple swelling on his left cheek. That eye was almost closed.

"Where are you going, Peter?" asked the woman.

"Osage," he mumbled, and Eugene saw too that his lower lip was swollen and split. "Soon's I get my horse and rig back from Henderson's."

He walked away up the street in the direction from which Eagle and Eugene had come. The woman watched him for a moment, then turned back toward the door. She paused with her hand on the knob. "Supper is at six."

"I'll be there, Emma," said Eagle.

"Your friend is welcome too."

Eagle started, and Eugene realized his presence had been forgotten.

"This here's John Miller," Eagle said then. "John, Emma Ashford. John's bunking with me till he gets a crib of his own."

Eugene felt her cool gray eyes in his boots. "I am pleased to make your acquaintance, John. Will you be dining with us?"

"John's making a delivery for Old Man Woodlawn down on the White. He won't be back in time for supper."

"That is unfortunate." Her smile was genuinely sad. "Isham, you know where the woodpile is."

When the door closed behind her, Eagle stirred. "Well, take down your roll, John, and come pick your corner. You ain't seen Sam Woodlawn mad till he's been kept waiting."

Eugene complied. Accompanying Eagle to the carriage house, he said: "She's pretty."

"That's what Terrence Ashford thought when he brung her here and had the good Christian sense to up and die and leave her the deed to a quarter of Springfield." The half-breed showed him his iron tooth. "Things go right at supper tonight, you get the bed out here."

CHAPTER SIX

Now, you and me, we schooled in French
and Holy Writ and sums;
But a barroom queen was Miller's bench—
his slate and blackboard guns.

April 10, 1855

Dear Eugene,

George Sharon gave me your letter, which you addressed to me in Ben Honey's care. The name "John Miller" puzzled me at first, but I know too well those lazy *l*'s and unclosed *o*'s I labored so hard to break you of when you attended school, and I let the hoe lie in the garden and supper boil over on the stove while I read your letter, the first word I have received in a year to tell me my oldest son is yet living.

I am happy that you have found work and that you have moved into your own quarters, as from what you wrote me about your friend Isham Eagle I do not consider him a healthy influence. You imagine that I cannot read between the lines when you write that he and the woman who owns the house he lives behind are friends, but in Wilmington someone would have seen to it that they were properly wed long ago. I do not lay any blame upon Mrs. Ashford, in whom I sense a woman of rare character; but in this man's world the woman who relies solely upon a male's whims and fancies is, as your grandfather would say, "treading water in a pond with no bottom." I fear for her welfare as I would for a sister's.

You asked how things are at home. An early frost last year killed most of the corn, but Henry was able to save twenty acres by borrowing skillets and turning them into smudgepots with hickory chips and smoldering rags. Your sister Maureen fell into a fever in February and for days her life was despaired of, but she has recovered completely. However, she is a grave child. She smiles rarely, laughs not at all, and when she looks at me I see deep mourning in her eyes, yet I am sure she does not remember her father and no longer grieves his loss. It is as if she has lived before and knows what sorrows and bitternesses await her. In all other respects she is normal and healthy.

Jerome has grown six inches since you left and is already Henry's match in labors on the farm. Matthew, whose hair is darkening, starts school in the fall. Your brothers miss you and keep asking when you will return.

Four days ago I baked a cake in honor of your birthday. I did this not from sentiment, but because I worried that Maureen would forget her oldest brother. You are thirteen now, no longer a boy, and responsible for your actions. All of life's great decisions are still before you. I have but your father's strength and the lessons I taught you to console me that you will face them, if not always with wisdom, then with direction and purpose. Evasion is simply a less honorable form of surrender.

I do not advise that you come home this spring. Owen Cook has friends in Waterloo, and opinion is evenly divided regarding the suitability or untimeliness of his cousin's death. Talk is of your arrest. George Sharon risked jail delivering your letter, whose possession, he informed me, could be considered evidence that he is concealing a fugitive. As much as it tears a mother's heart, I must ask that you remain away and do not write again except in matters of urgency, as letters are easily traced to their authors.

I will address this to "John Miller, Springfield, Missouri," and give it to Mr. Sharon to send with his next shipment south.

Your loving mother

"Miller! Come lend a hand!"

Standing in the dirty light sliding in through the oiled paper over the storeroom window, Eugene blinked himself back from Iowa. Sam Woodlawn's bawl was enough to set the food tins and liniment bottles buzzing on the shelves. He folded the paper carefully, preserving his mother's creases, stuck it away inside his jacket, and went outdoors, where his bearded employer stood glaring at one of his gray mules with its rump on the ground in front of the delivery wagon. As Eugene approached, the animal peeled back its upper lip and brayed. This was the mule he had privately named Curly.

"I'd shoot the son of a bitch," Woodlawn said, "but then the other'n'd start acting up. The innuns believe when one animal dies its soul passes into another, and I commence to think they're right, the onion-skinned bastards."

"Give me your pipe," Eugene said.

"My which?"

He repeated the demand, holding out his palm. After staring at it a moment, the man removed the short-stemmed corncob he had burning perilously close to his whiskers and surrendered it. Eugene inserted it between his own teeth, not inhaling, while he wrapped his bandanna kerchief around the thumb and forefinger of his left hand. Then he squatted, knocked the glowing dottle of tobacco out on to the ground, and picked it up in the kerchief.

"Ready with those reins," he told Woodlawn, standing.

The former mountain man took up the slack while Eugene approached the mule, the wrapped hand hidden. It stopped making noise to turn its head and glare at him with one walleye. When its lip skinned back for another defiant blast Eugene shoved the red-hot coal directly into its right nostril.

The bray turned into a shriek, and the mule bounded to its feet, shaking its head and snorting desperately. At the same instant Woodlawn leaned the reins taut, his grapefruit-muscles bulging. Meanwhile Eugene swiftly secured the traces between animal and wagon, and by the time the mule had cleared its nose of the angry stinging thing it was in no position to balk again.

Woodlawn let the reins drop and examined the animal's muzzle. Most of the hair inside and the skin around the nostril had burned away. When he touched fingers to the injury the mule squealed and tried to bite his hand. He jerked it back.

"Hard way to use a beast," was his only comment.

Eugene said, "You don't fool around with a bad mule. Not and live."

"Well, iffen that burn takes to infecting it's your dog to kick. This load goes to St. Louis."

"That's a two-week round trip!" protested Eugene.

"Nearer three. You're bringing back a load of chiny, and every cup you bust you buy."

"Pelts going out?"

"Bear and elk. Cured and tanned and ready for wear. The plew."

"Bandits?"

"Nothing a mule-burner like you can't handle."

"I'll need someone along."

Woodlawn's scalp scar reddened. "Eagle runs off with this rig you bought that too."

"Who said Eagle?"

"You made any other friends since you come to town?"

"I made some."

Emma Ashford was one, if you called that sort of thing being friends. His first three nights in Springfield, Eugene had had the bed in the carriage house to himself. The third night, a good hour after Isham Eagle and the widow would have finished supper, Eugene had sneaked out and into the main house through the back door, which he found open. He had been impressed with the size of the rooms and their furniture, particularly a big piano with a propped-open lid that took up the space of three of the upright boxes he had seen on trips to Waterloo. The ground floor was dark, as were the stairs leading to the second story when he found and opened that door. He had crept up the stairs to a carpeted hallway washed in silver starlight through a window at the end and had taken one step along it when he heard an exclamation and froze.

He thought at first he'd been discovered. But the hallway in front of him was deserted and when he turned he found that he was alone at the top of the staircase. Then there had been another exclamation, breathy, female. He thought it had come from behind one of the doors in the hallway. He took off his boots and tiptoed in stockinged feet to the one he suspected. There, for the next ten minutes, he stood listening to the noises of love, to girlish mews and mannish grunts and one long tinkling scream that lifted the hairs on the back of his neck. Silence followed, then a murmur of conversation he couldn't make out. He picked up his boots and went back down and out to the carriage house, where he lay awake much of the night.

The noises were not new to him. He had heard similar ones up in his loft, coming from the ground floor of the house in Iowa. Then, however, they had seemed shameful, and eerily unlike his parents' austere natures. But it was not shame that denied him sleep that third night in Springfield.

Later, weeks after he had moved his meager possessions into a rooming house down the street, he had gone back to the carriage house looking for Eagle's companionship. One of the big front doors was open and Emma Ashford stood on the threshold sweeping clouds of dust out into the yard. When she saw Eugene she smiled, the same smile she had showed him when they were introduced. She was wearing a pearl-colored dress that picked up her gray eyes and the color in her cheeks at the same time. Tiny pale buttons drew an unbroken line from her waist over her bosom to her throat.

"Hello, John. Isham is out riding, if you're looking for him. He took along a fishing pole, so I don't think he will be back before supper. He has a secret fishing hole. It is five miles north, on Herb Clutter's farm."

He found his tongue. "I guess it ain't much of a secret."

"Isn't." She touched fingers to her lips. "I apologize. Isham's grammar is hideous and I am always correcting him."

He couldn't think of anything to say to that. He realized he was staring at her. She glanced down at the broom and gave a nervous laugh.

"He is also a terrible housekeeper. I let my girl go months ago. They carry tales."

Again he said nothing. He wished desperately that he were like the Arkansas drummer, with a story for every pause. Mrs. Ashford laughed again and brushed an auburn hair back from her forehead. Then she was serious.

"You did come to see Isham?"

"Well, who else?" he said after a moment. And in the saying, realized it was a lie.

Her eyes flickered down to his boots and up again. "Isham said you are thirteen. You are small for that age."

"I reckon." He stopped himself just short of apologizing for his lack of size.

"You are sturdy, however. You have a mature build for one so young."

"Well, from all that loading and unloading."

"I imagine young ladies admire you."

He didn't shrug, though he wanted to. His success at being ignored by the minimal female population of Springfield had thus far been complete.

"Have you had luncheon?"

He had; but he said no. After another little silence she put away the broom and they went into the main house.

Now, months later, he remembered mainly the trouble he had had with all those buttons.

To Sam Woodlawn, he said: "Isham Eagle's a good man with a gun. If he steals anything I'll pay for it."

"Miller, I didn't need to be told that." The old mountain man recharged his pipe. "Fetch me some axle grease for this here burn and go pull that breed offen the widder. You want to make the Gasconade by dark."

He found Eagle splitting firewood behind the carriage house and they agreed to divide Eugene's wages for the trip to St. Louis and back. The half-breed had sweated through his flannels top, and his hard, hairless pectorals showed through the drenched material. Eugene helped him carry wood up to the house. Mrs. Ashford came out while they were dumping it into the box outside the back door.

"Emma, me and John's going to St. Louis for Old Man Woodlawn. Be back next month."

"Do you need anything?"

"Well, nothing I can take along." The iron tooth spoiled Eagle's bright grin.

"Will you write?"

"I ain't much for that."

"John?" She was looking at Eugene now.

Eugene felt Eagle's surprise. "We'll beat any letters back," he mumbled.

"Yes, I keep forgetting how slow the communication is out here."

She smoothed her dress. "Be watchful, both of you. There are bandits in the hills."

Eagle borrowed provisions from her and took along his revolving rifle and Walker Colt, storing them in the wagon bed behind the seat while laying the Navy on the seat between himself and Eugene, who drove. Eugene wore his Colt's Paterson under his jacket, slung from a piece of thick twine he had stitched inside. He had found carrying it under his belt uncomfortable when driving. They had gone several miles before Eagle spoke.

"You ought to lose that Paterson, get yourself a real gun."

"What's wrong with it?"

"Nothing, so long as you don't stir up more'n six men at a time. You got to take the barrel off to reload and meantime old number seven's weighting you down with lead from a Dragoon."

"Well, what's best?"

Eagle lit a cheroot, deep in thought. "I like the Navy. Some don't, on account of that thirty-six caliber, which don't always do the job, although I ain't had nobody come back to complain. The Walker and the Dragoon pistol get the job done every time, but they're saddle guns and a little rabbit like you'd get so tuckered just carrying them around you couldn't lift them when it counted. I seen a man in Kansas month before last had him a neat little gun you can put in your pocket, a English piece, only I don't know where you'd go to look for one. Also it was double-action and when you fire them things without cocking first the old cap gets caught and jams the cylinder." He flicked off a quarter-inch of ash without removing the cheroot from between his lips. "I reckon you got to keep looking till you find the one that's right for you."

Eugene drove on, unsatisfied.

They talked little the rest of the day, a situation that suited Eugene normally, but that was unusual for Eagle. From time to time the youth would feel his companion's eyes on him, only to find him staring straight ahead when he turned to meet his gaze. He was very aware of the revolver on the seat between them.

That night, while they were camping on the Gasconade River, Eugene came up the bank, shaking drops of water out of the tin plate he had just washed, and found Eagle watching him from his side of the fire. Rosy light from the flames twitched and crawled over his narrow Indian features where he sat on a rotting log. In that light his eyes looked less like a white man's.

"Emma likes you," he said.

Eugene wrapped the plate in a towel with the nap worn off and put it in the wagon. "That straight?"

"She ain't your usual kind of woman. When she likes you she does something about it."

"That straight?" he repeated. He had his back to Eagle, his hand on the gun inside his jacket. Through it he could feel the vibration of his heart.

Eagle said, "I do some moving around. I ain't no tramp, though. The reason I ain't no tramp is I got me a place to come back to. I'd be powerful mad I was to lose it."

Eugene made a quarter turn toward him. His hand was still inside his jacket, in shadow. "Hell, Ish, if that's what's biting you, I got a place. I don't want yours."

"I seen that look Emma give you. I ain't stupid just because I'm half Indian."

"Ish, I ain't after your place."

"It ain't good enough?"

"Good enough's got nothing to do with it. Every time I chop wood I got to count my toes before and after."

Eagle was quiet for a long time, his eyes on his companion. Then: "Yeah?"

"It's pitiful."

The iron tooth gleamed. The barrel of the Navy pointed skyward and the hammer came down gently. He had been holding it level the whole time, in shadow. "They ain't no trick to it," he said, putting away the weapon. "It's all in the rhythm of your swing."

Eugene smiled then and took his hand off the Paterson. The pair turned in.

CHAPTER SEVEN

Some say he rode with Lincoln's blue,
others, Stonewall Jack;
Down Misery way, they claim it's true,
the flag he bore was black.

The trip took eight days. No one accosted them the first seven, and Eugene was starting to get less watchful when they encountered four riders the morning of the last. One called out Eagle's name and came up on the gallop. His beard was ginger-colored, almost red, and sunburn had peeled a small Irish nose and cheeks whose rose-petal fairness reminded Eugene of a girl's. He grasped Eagle's outstretched hand eagerly. Eugene placed him in his mid-twenties. He and his companions were dressed in heavy coats and old hats and straddling hollow-flanked mounts with rifles behind the cantles.

"Quill, how the hell are you?" said the half-breed.

"Well, I still got my scalp, and nobody's tried hanging me lately." The newcomer's eyes took in the wagon and team. They were Wedgwood blue, the whites shot with blood. "You look to prosper."

"This trip I'm just shotgun. Meet my partner, John Miller. John, Jim Quill, the best liar in Missouri."

"There's lots better. But none louder." His teeth shone white in the ginger overgrowth. "You voting?"

"Voting on what?"

"Slavery. Hell, ain't you heard? This here's election day."

"How much they paying this time?"

"Ten dollars gold to vote yes. We all voted three times, except for Israel there, who only voted twice. He's the honest one."

Eugene couldn't tell which one was Israel. Quill's companions were to a man dark and unshaven and in need of a bath. They could not raise a smile among them.

The two conversed for a few minutes, mostly about men whose colorful names the youth didn't recognize. "It was good seeing you, Quill," Eagle said then.

"You see?" Quill twinkled at Eugene. "I'm anything but the best."

The parties continued in opposite directions. When Quill and the others were out of earshot, Eugene said: "I'm glad you knew each other. I thought for sure they were bandits."

"They are."

Entering St. Louis, Eugene felt grateful for having seen and got to know Springfield before coming here, or he'd have fallen down dead from its sheer hugeness. It fanned out on both sides of the broad Missouri, a patchwork quilt of wooden and brick buildings constructed in proper blocks under its own cloud of wood- and coal-smoke, a black umbrella that hung motionless over the city. He had never handled a team in such heavy traffic; when, having followed the complicated directions of a pedestrian with a French accent, he came at last to his destination, he was holding the reins so tight he had to peel them away like a bandage to avoid skinning his hands. His ears shrank from the cacophony raised by wagons and human voices.

"Is it always like this?" he shouted to Eagle, helping him unload the baled pelts.

"Just during the week. Saturdays it gets busy."

The buyer, a very fat Englishman whose vest crept up to expose an acre of white linen, inspected the bales swiftly, riffling the pelts like playing cards. Then he wrote out a receipt and gave it to Eugene and asked him to come back the next day for the china Woodlawn had ordered. "I shall have someone see to your team. The Golden West, around the corner, offers commendable lodgings at a fair rate."

"What's fair?"

The Englishman tugged at a curled moustache with a pudgy hand. "A dollar."

"A week?"

"A day."

Walking away with Eagle, Eugene asked him how people managed to live in St. Louis.

"It's just during the election." Eagle steered him around a small woman in a broadcloth cape trailing a black slave loaded down with packages. "Lots of folks in from Illinois and Kansas to cast ballots."

"They come all the way from Kansas for ten dollars?"

"It's probably twenty if you prove you come from there. And then if there's a rich abolitionist handy you might could get him to bid it up. This here's the Golden West. I used to stay here for two bits back when it was the Napoleon."

"Sorry, gents. Full up."

The clerk behind the counter in the brocaded lobby was built thick, with hair so fair and fine it appeared to be floating away from his pink face. He spoke with an accent that Eugene decided was true Virginian. Eagle looked him over quickly and said, "What's the matter, can't a fellow from out West get a place to cool leather in this here town?"

"You're from Kansas?" The clerk pursed his lips.

"You hear the one about the Missouri farmer that moved to Arkansas and raised the intelligence of both states?"

"Sorry. We have them waiting three deep now for rooms that won't become available before next week."

"That's sore to hear. Me and twenny-six others just rid in from Leavenworth to vote down them damn abolitionists. The rest set up camp outside town, but me and my little brother here got other business so we're looking for a roof to stretch our legs under. But if a good proslaver can't find hospitality I reckon we might just as soon all vote to free the niggers."

"One moment, sir." The clerk said *suh*. He went through a door behind the counter, to return less than a minute later with a key.

"The manager is back East on business," he explained, placing the key on the counter. "He is a Georgia native and if he were here I am confident he would offer you the use of his own room during the emergency, as I am doing. The regular dollar rate will be sufficient."

Eugene paid him out of the money Woodlawn had advanced him, and the clerk directed the pair to the manager's quarters on the ground floor, where they dropped their bedrolls.

"Quill was right," said the youth. "He isn't the best liar in Missouri."

Eagle, stretched out on the comfortable bed, grinned. He was the most expressionable savage his companion had ever heard tell of. "I

could of got it free-no-charge," he said. "But I didn't want to push
the mule so hard it sat on me."

He went to sleep almost immediately. Eugene, wide awake and
restless, let himself out quietly and left the hotel to explore new
ground. On his way through the lobby he was hailed by the clerk.
"Going out to bring in your friends?"

"Uh, yes," replied the youth. "Them damn abolitionists get their
way, we'll all of us be voting side by side with niggers next election."

Actually, Eugene had never thought one way or the other about
Negroes. He and Henry had got along well enough in Iowa. Now that
he was employed and part of the free-enterprise system, he suspected
that all that free labor in the slave states had a lot to do with why the
northern abolitionists wanted it stopped.

The streets were teeming. He kept a thumb hooked inside the
pocket containing his expense money and ducked into available door-
ways to breathe. When it came to crowds a youth or a man of less
than usual height had to take his oxygen where he could. He found
the stores stocked with all kinds of exotic merchandise unobtainable
in either Waterloo or Springfield, and admired a red-and-green Na-
vajo blanket his mother would appreciate. He jingled the coins in his
pocket, wondering what Sam Woodlawn would say to his borrowing
business money for a personal gift. At length he decided he knew
what he would say, and to do some more looking around until he had
the sand to face it.

One doorway took him into a building that was all one big room,
with white plank floors and a chalk-smeared blackboard at the far end.
Through the shifting crowd inside, he glimpsed two rows of oak desks
with benches attached and realized he had wandered into a school-
house where voting was going on. He was pushing his way back toward the street when shouting broke out behind him. Curious, he
turned just in time to see metal flash through a gap in the crowd.
Someone gasped.

"He's cut!" said a voice.

More shouts, pushing and shoving. Eugene's way out was blocked
by men fighting their way in to get a look at the brawl. Among them
was a big man in a blue uniform and round cap with a shiny visor. He
was holding a varnished oak stick, which he used as a lever to pry his
way through the press of bodies. A path opened before him. Through

it, Eugene saw two men grappling; one had a stained knife in a hand whose wrist was held fast in the other's clenched fingers. The stick arced down. Both men howled and the knife clattered to the floor. (Eugene never found out if the policeman had aimed for the wrist or the hand holding it.) The pair parted, and the youth saw that the second man was bleeding, the stain spreading along his white cotton sleeve like wine on a tablecloth in Springfield's best restaurant.

"What's it about?" demanded the policeman. He had fierce black handlebars and a chin as blue as his coat.

"Women, what else?" called a voice from the crowd. Knowing laughter swept through it.

The man in uniform looked from one of the brawlers to the other. "Which one's the abolitionist?"

"I am," said the bleeding man. He was grasping the injured arm above the elbow.

"You vote yet?"

"I was fixing to, when this son of a—"

"You're under arrest."

The bleeding man gaped. "Me? What for?"

"Disturbing the peace and using profanity in a public place." Hooking his stick on his belt, the policeman twisted a hand in the man's shirt collar and swung him toward the doorway and steamed him toward it, grasping his belt in back. Hoots of laughter dogged them. Just before the gap closed behind the pair, Eugene saw the other grappler pick up his knife and wipe the blade on his trousers, grinning.

The youth had seen enough of St. Louis. He found his way out and started across the street toward the hotel. In the middle he waited for a brewer's dray to trundle past. When the way was clear he looked at Devil Cook standing in front of him.

He was a year older, but unchanged: lean almost to the point of emaciation, darker than Isham Eagle, though he was white, the coarse flesh of his cheeks divided by twin scars as pale as maggots. He had on the same weathered pinch-crowned hat he had worn on the expedition to Nebraska City, and faded homespun that might have been the same, his narrow waist encircled by an army belt with a curved maple butt showing above the holster and the flap unbuttoned and tucked inside the belt. He saw Eugene at the same time Eugene saw him, but

to him recognition came more slowly; and that was the youth's first
indication that he himself had changed.

"Gene Morner," was all Cook said.

The name chilled him as no blasphemy could. He had not been
called by it for a year. And while he was calling it, Cook was scooping
the gun with the maple butt out of his holster. Eugene's own hand
went inside his jacket, with a resigned sort of movement made
smooth by the knowledge that it was going to be years too late.

The report was loud and nasty and splattered the noise of the street
like a rock hurled through a big window. Eugene flinched, feeling the
bullet go in. And saw Devil Cook arch and the revolver turn upside-
down on the end of his trigger finger and slide off and hit the street in
a puff of yellow dust that was still settling when the gun's owner
smothered it with his body. He placed both his palms flat on the
street as if trying to push himself back up. Then he settled, his face in
the dust.

Any gap his narrow form might have left in the townscape was
filled by Isham Eagle, standing in front of the boardwalk that ran past
the hotel with his right foot in front of his left and his right arm still
outstretched at shoulder level, ending in his Navy Colt. The last of
the smoke left the muzzle in a skybound patch. Only when it had
cleared his vision did he lower the weapon and come forward to stand
over the dead scout. By then a crowd was gathering.

"You all of a piece?" he asked Eugene, his eyes still on the body.

The youth inspected his front for holes. He was holding the Paterson at last. "I reckon. I thought it was him shooting."

"Took you for somebody else, did he?"

They were looking at each other now. Eagle had overheard Cook.
Eugene said, "Yes."

They were joined by the big policeman, who glared from the body
to Eagle. "What?"

"Abolitionist," the youth said quickly. "He put a gun on me."

The policeman swung his handlebars on Eugene. The whites of his
eyes were pink. "He vote yet?"

"I reckon that's where he was headed."

"Anybody here to say it wasn't justified?" Bloodshot eyes scanned
the crowd, which held silence. He pointed his stick at Eagle, then at
Eugene. "You and you. Stop in to the station later and tell the cap'n

what you told me. Clear out, the rest of you. This ain't no public hanging."

Eagle belted the Navy and came over to stand by the youth while the policeman was dispersing the crowd. "Well, anyway, that's how it's done."

"I sure can't go home now." It was a mumble.

"What?"

"It ain't worth repeating," said John Miller, and went back to the Golden West.

Jim Quill came to Springfield in the fall of 1856, in the company of the same three dark men with whom young Miller had first seen him, and another man, older, with great swooping black moustaches and eyes set so far back under the shelf of his brows they looked like candles burning in a cave. His hat was blocked strangely, the brim flat on one side, swept up on the other, and decorated with a plume dyed bright red. He wore a military-style greatcoat brass-buttoned to the neck, with insignia on the shoulders. The alligator butt of an odd revolver curved out of his belt where the coat split in front.

They dismounted and tied up in front of the Ozark General Merchandise, where John Miller—longer in the jaw now and sporting a dusky growth on his upper lip, but only two inches taller than he had been at twelve—was scrubbing soot off the front window with a sponge and a bucket of brackish water. They walked past him without looking his way, spurs jingling like loose change, and went inside. He tossed the sponge into the bucket and followed them.

"Something I can do for you, Mr. Quill?" he asked. "The owner's home sick today." Actually, Sam Woodlawn was sleeping off a jug of trade whiskey, an abomination whose ingredients included chewing tobacco and kerosene, to which he had become addicted during his mountaineering days. It happened once a month—twice in December, in honor of the Lord's birth—and young Miller had earned enough of his employer's trust to run the business until his recovery.

His gun slung, he was unprepared for the speed with which the man in the greatcoat whirled on him, snaking out his revolver and thumbing back the hammer. Miller found himself looking down two short barrels, over and under, the bottom one nearly large enough to put his thumb inside. Slowly he moved his hands away from his body, palms out, and held them there.

Quill said, "Where you know my name from, son?"

"St. Lou." He watched the man in the greatcoat, who was sighting along the top barrel at the space between his eyes. "Election day last year. Isham Eagle introduced us."

Eagle's ginger-bearded acquaintance stepped closer and peered into the youth's face. "The kid, yeah. Smith, weren't it?"

"Miller. John Miller."

"Lay down your hackles, Major. He's a friend of Eagle's."

"He has a gun under his coat."

"Well, hell, who don't? But I reckon if he come in looking to use his, it'd be in his hand."

Nothing in the stranger's face changed. It was all harsh edges and black hollows, like a rock wall cut by glaciers. Finally the gun arm bent and the hammer came down gently. He returned the weapon to his belt.

Quill said, "Miller, this here is Major Charles Foosh. He's with the Missouri militia."

"Fouché," corrected the man in the greatcoat. His mouth was completely hidden beneath his moustaches, and but for a slight stirring of the hairs it might have been someone else speaking.

"I didn't know we had a militia," said Miller.

"It is high time one was established."

"Know where we can find Eagle?" Quill asked.

"Depends what you want him for."

"Well, we figure it's something he'll like."

Miller directed them then to Emma Ashford's house. Quill thanked him and led the way out. The glowing pinpoints in the shadow of Major Fouché's brow lingered on the youth a moment before he turned and followed.

The old woman who ran the rooming house where Miller lived met him just inside the door when he returned that evening. "Men t'see you," she bellowed. Because she was deaf, she acted as if everyone else shared that disability. "Showed 'em up t'the room. That Isham Eagle is with them."

Her tone was full of her judgment of Eagle. Miller nodded and went upstairs, transferring the Colt's Paterson from the sling inside his jacket to his pocket and leaving his hand in with it. He had an idea who the men were and did not want to be caught naked a second time.

"John, I reckon you know Jim Quill and Major Foosh," said Eagle, getting up from Miller's bed.

"Fouché." The Major was standing by the window, holding back the curtain to see out. Although the room was warm, he had retained his plumed hat and greatcoat.

"We met." Miller kept his hand in his pocket.

Eagle was grinning. "Well, Jim done me a service by introducing me, and I'm passing on his good works. Jim, you tell it."

But it was not Quill, stretching his legs out in the room's only chair and poking new holes in the threadbare rug with his spurs, who spoke. "Last month the Jayhawkers fired a farmer's house and barn in Jasper County and knew his wife by force," the Major said. "His son was shot but he lives."

"I heard. It was in answer to the Lawrence raid." In May of that year, a guerrilla band led by Missouri proslavers had invaded Lawrence, Kansas, and killed every male they encountered, boy and man.

"Vengeance is the business of God."

Quill said, "We're fixing to ride back Kansas way and deal them damn abolitionists a card offen the same deck."

"Sounds mighty like the business of God."

"Missouri must be protected," said Fouché. "Our duty is to demonstrate to the world that its borders may not be violated with impunity."

"The world being Kansas."

"In this case, yes."

"What's it got to do with me and Ish?"

Eagle said, "That's Sergeant Eagle to you. You can be one too, you want. See, that's how come I brung them here."

Miller looked at the three, and at the silent dark trio slouching like tired fixtures against the walls. "Hell, Ish, what do we care what these proslavers do? You and me never kept a slave in our lives."

"Well, who has, that we know? It'll be a hoot. We'll just hooraw them Kansas boys a little and get out. Major's paying good wages."

"The Major's a rich man," Quill said. "His maw owns a witchhazel plant in Philadelphia."

"Rubbing compounds and coal oil," clarified the Major. "The refinery belongs to my grandfather, but he is incapacitated and my mother pays the help."

"She know what you do with your allowance?"

Fouché turned from the window. His eyes were invisible. "It was not my wish to come here. Lieutenant Quill assured me that Eagle is handy with firearms and Eagle gave you the same recommendation. I do not recruit infants."

"John's little, but good," Eagle put in. "A natural-born gun man."

"I am nothing if not fair. We shall test him in the field."

"John?"

The youth jerked his chin. "What kind of gun's that?"

"This?" The Major took out the revolver with the checked butt. Miller's finger touched the trigger in his pocket, relaxing when Fouché turned his gun sideways. "It is brand new, designed by Dr. Le Mat of New Orleans. It fires a regular ball and a round of shot. You select barrels by adjusting the nose of the hammer."

Miller fingered the Paterson a moment longer. Then he took his hand out empty. "I want one."

"Should we come to an understanding, I shall send back for another."

Isham Eagle clapped his hands. "Let's get drunk and seal it."

The Major said, "I am temperance."

CHAPTER EIGHT

Four years by war that state was rent,
a death for every knell;
And them that asked where Miller went
was told to start in hell.

The historic "siege" of Topeka by Fouché's Raiders, as the Missouri militia would be known, was the first of those that would settle on its commander the name Slaughtering Charley Foosh in the abolitionist press, or Charley Slaughter, as constant use would simplify it. The proslavery newspapers in Leavenworth and Atchison and throughout Missouri referred to him by his military title until Sumter fell and the columns grew heavy with more legitimate rank. After that, the friendly press tried dubbing him Fire-Eating Charley, in answer to the Union's General Joseph "Fighting Joe" Hooker; but as casualties mounted and the glittering War for Southern Independence dragged on into the cancer of civil war, the hated (by the Major) epithet began to appear even there. In later years, the name Major Charles Fouché would meet only blank stares in Springfield, while the mere mention of Charley Slaughter would provoke fistfights in the gentlest assemblies.

Other names came out of the Topeka raid, their owners to remain for years in that eye with which the public views rebels, bandits, and the odd assassin: James Monroe Quill, who would stand trial after Appomattox for the rape-murder of the daughter of an abolitionist newspaperman, and hang; the Stark brothers, Matthew, Luke, and Israel, who would be shot to pieces by a citizen's vigilance committee in 1874 while robbing a Leavenworth bank visited two days earlier by the James Gang; their cousin Samson, later a Missouri state representative, in which office he would in 1877 take four bullets fired by a

friend of one of his cousins' victims, all of them fatal; and Isham
Eagle, a Cherokee half-breed from the Nations and commonly ac-
knowledged inventor of the fast draw of fiction and song, from whom
history would hear more. Witnesses to that first raid would be at a loss
to identify three others captured after Lee's surrender, two of them
forgotten by posterity, the third little more than a boy in that October of 1856, when four Kansans went to their Creator and nine hundred dollars in gold went from a freight office safe into the Missouri
militia's treasury. As John Miller was to say whenever someone
pumped him about it later: "It's all there in the books. Look it up
your ownself."

The morning after his return from Kansas, Miller reported to work
and found Sam Woodlawn entrenched behind the counter, leaning
on his knuckles on the sawdust-strewn top. His beard was in tangles
and his eyes were scored around red, but he appeared steady, the rock
around which, literally, the store had been built. It took more than a
two-day drunk to put him down.

"How you feeling, Mr. Woodlawn?"

"How was Topeka?"

Miller finished tying on his gunnysack apron without pausing. "I
never been."

"Buffalo shit. This town's full of mouths and every one of them is
flapping."

"Well, they're all wrong."

"You're fired."

The youth glared. "Ain't you going to listen to my side of it?"

"I give you the chance. You lied. Get out."

"What if I did go? I never heard you claim to be for abolition."

"I ain't. I was a slave once of the Blackfeet out of my own damn
foolishness. It's the natural way of things when you come up short in
the balance. But I got to trade with both sides here and when it gets
out I'm paying a border raider I'll lose half my business. That's if the
Jayhawkers don't come riding in and burn me out first."

Miller took off his apron and slapped it down on the counter.
"Give me my time."

The grizzled merchant counted out coins from the collar box where
he kept his silver. "Count it again," he said.

"Ain't necessary." Miller pocketed the money and turned to leave.

Woodlawn said, "You stay away from Isham Eagle and them, I might could take you back on in a month or two. After the talking's quit."

"The Major pays better."

"Pays in lead, you mean. Them days is past when you can ride hell for leather over God and the law and expect it won't catch up with you. You set fire to both ends of a powder trail and you'll come to running around in circles tighter and tighter and blow up in the middle. I seed it happen."

"Well," said Miller, "the boom will be something to hear."

"What do you care?" The old mountain man's face was a fierce totem strung with hair. "You won't hear it."

The boom made by Miller's new Le Mat was loud enough when he fired shot out the smooth lower barrel, peppering a can of lard perched in the crotch of a sycamore so that the pale congealed grease oozed out like limp porcupine quills. With a father's proprietary pride, the man who had given it to him stepped up and showed him how to adjust the nose of the hammer so he could make use of the other barrel, then stood back while the youth clipped a twig off a maple clothed in glorious fall color thirty yards away. The Major grunted approval.

"That is about as far as you may expect it to be accurate." He watched Miller change hands on the gun and shake circulation back into his fingers. "You will get used to the recoil. The weapon takes a larger ball than you are accustomed to firing."

It was unusually warm for November, and Fouché had his coat unbuttoned for the first time in their acquaintance. The little clearing in the woods north of Springfield was littered with punctured cans and the shattered corpses of a hundred bottles. The Missouri militia, eleven strong now, had been using it for meetings and target practice for a month. The Major, having hidden the nine hundred dollars seized from the freight office in Topeka, had scrupulously recorded the amount in a leather-bound notebook and was paying his soldiers out of it at the rate of four dollars per man per week, noting the outgo each time. For the Starks, not long out of the deep Ozark country to the south, these were better wages than they had known, not counting their bandit past, now piously recanted. For Jim Quill and Isham Eagle and John Miller, they were better than a man could expect for just busting caps and generally staying within earshot of the Major whenever he wanted to review them.

At the moment, Miller and Fouché were alone, and as the youth drew from the cotton sack of big lead balls his commander had provided and from his own leather patch studded with copper caps, he was conscious of the Major's silence. Unlike Eagle, the man in the plumed hat was not talkative, and like all quiet men his vocabulary of silences was vast. This one was working up to something.

"Sergeant Miller," he began.

Miller looked up from the powder he was measuring into the Le Mat's chambers. He tolerated the military title, which seemed bogus without a uniform to go with it; but the Major's tailor was in Philadelphia.

Fouché went on. "I have lived in Missouri two years. I came here directly from the Harvard School of Law, to which I submitted for no other reason than to please my mother. I enjoy the life, nature's raw beauty and the physical separation from the suffocating statutes I was forced to commit to memory during those four gray years. However, the, er, lack of female companionship is, er, trying. There is, I am told, an establishment in Springfield, but I have the delicacy of my position to—" He broke off, his face as red as his plume. "Oh, but you are just a boy!"

Miller grinned. "I'll introduce you, Major. 'Course, if it's delicate you're after, you might want to change out of that uniform first."

The Major assumed a martial stance. "I withdraw my comment. Decidedly, you are not a boy."

"There ain't any boys in Missouri."

"Tonight, then." He buttoned his greatcoat, and when that was done it was as if the conversation hadn't happened. He picked up the riddled lard can and tied it to the end of a thong he had knotted to a branch of the sycamore. "Reload the shotgun barrel," he ordered, setting the can swinging. "Let us see how you are with a moving target."

Moving targets were no problem, as Miller proved the following spring, when the militia stirred itself to fire a community of half-finished log cabins being built by abolitionist emigrants from Atchison. One enraged settler, although surprised on foot, managed his horse with the aid of the scudding smoke and charged Miller, yelling and whirling the ax he had been using to notch logs. The youth waited astride his Cheyenne roan until the horse was close enough to reach out and lay a hand on, then released a full load of shot from the Le Mat into his attacker's face. He saw the pellets go in, then a sheet of blood came down like a curtain over the man's features and his terrified mount peeled off, the thing on its back swaying from side to side until it toppled off into the foundation of the flaming cabin. One other settler was killed in the skirmish and Luke Stark lost an ear to a close blast from a proper shotgun.

Summer followed, its cloying stillness disturbed just once, when a small band of Jayhawkers seeking vengeance for Topeka and the burned settlement stumbled upon Isham Eagle at his secret fishing hole on Herb Clutter's farm and shot him three times in the back. Left for dead, he crawled the mile and a half to the house, where a doctor dug out two balls, patched the holes where a third had gone through high on the shoulder, and advised the Clutters to make him as comfortable as possible during his last days.

"John, do you find my limbs attractive?" Peeling aside the cotton coverlet, Emma Ashford stretched a round naked leg ceilingward. Lamplight reflected off the whiteness of her thigh. Outside, a moth as big as a bat hurled itself at the window screen.

Miller, seated on the edge of the mattress, working his thumbnail under a spike in the sole of his boot, glanced at the leg. "What do you care? They're covered all day."

"If I felt that way, I'd not spend so much on petticoats." She raised the other leg and frowned at them both, her hands linked behind her knees for support.

"They're all right."

"'All right' is for cows and horses." She lowered them. "Did you visit Isham today?"

"I will tomorrow. He just lays there on his belly and don't say nothing."

"Doesn't say anything. Will he die, do you think?"

"Major's waiting on that to decide him on what we do back to them Jayhawkers and how much." The spike head was starting to loosen. The point had been pricking him all day.

"If he lives, what will you tell him about us?"

"What about us?"

She hesitated. "Terrence's study has not been touched since he died. There is an inch of dust on the desk. If I cleaned it, it would be a place for you to retreat those times when you have had your surfeit of me. I know the value men place on their privacy."

Terrence Ashford was her late husband. Miller said, "I got a room. What do I need with another?"

"I own the dry goods," she said, affecting not to have heard him. "I will retire Oscar Nordsen with a pension and you will manage the business in his place. It does not do for the man not to work. There will be talk enough about the difference in our ages without that."

The spike came free suddenly and flew across the room, tinkling down behind the chiffonier.

Later, turning over, Miller stared at the stylized toy soldiers printed on the wallpaper, rows and rows of little men marching in the moonlight banking through the window, each exactly the same as his neighbor. When he closed his eyes he could still see them. Just before dawn he climbed carefully out of bed, waited to hear the woman's measured breathing, then went out, carrying his now spikeless boots. He put them on in the hallway where, three years ago, a boy had crouched listening to the sounds of love. Then he left in that way that men leave places to which they do not intend to return.

He had not returned by January of 1858, when fourteen men, a slat-thin Isham Eagle among them, walked their horses with hoofs bound in rags through six inches of fresh snow to a rise overlooking a camp of Jayhawkers stopped two miles east of Independence. The Kansans were on their way back home with a string of horses stolen from a breeder near Boonville. But for the horses picketed nearby, their blanket-wrapped forms might have been logs scattered in the snow.

"Cold camp," observed the Major, in a theatrical whisper. "Was there ever proof more damning than the consuming fear of a man's own guilt, that will not allow him a fire on a freezing night?" Although there was no moon, the snow's own ghostly blue illumination painted rectangles of shadow on the rough-hewn face.

Miller decided against reminding him that they themselves had not struck a match since leaving Springfield, and bent with the others to unwrap his mount's hoofs. Rising, he saw Eagle sway and put a hand on his Appaloosa's side to steady himself. The horse flinched, flirting its head.

"All right, Ish?" Miller whispered.

"Hell no, I ain't all right. I been shot. I'll live, though."

Luke Stark shushed him. The darkest of the three brothers, he still wore a white bandage to cover the place where his right ear had been shot off, although it had been healed for some time.

The order to mount hissed through the ranks. Jim Quill did so and drew his weapon, one of the new Smith & Wesson revolvers with a self-contained cartridge, nearly as long as Eagle's Walker Colt, which the half-breed left in his saddle scabbard while he swung a leg over and unbelted the Navy. Stepping into leather, Miller rested the Paterson on his thigh while he checked the eight loads in the Le Mat's cylinder. Eagle watched him.

"How you figure to work two pistols and steer your horse too?" he demanded.

Grinning, Miller clamped the reins between his teeth. He had broken—or rebroken—the roan to saddle and had long since discarded the horsehair rig for a proper bridle.

"That damn Cheyenne horse has got to your head," said Eagle.

They charged the camp with a rebel yell that shattered the brittle cold air and had Jayhawkers scrambling to disentangle themselves from their blankets. To his uniform the Major had added an officer's saber, which he slashed at the squirming bundles to right and left, the blade glistening dark on the upswings. Miller fired his revolvers in a hammering rhythm at other bundles and at upright figures who had managed to clear themselves, and some went down, but in the fog of spent breath and smoke from his weapons and those of his companions he was unable to keep count. When the Colt's clicked empty he belted it, and when he had fired the last chamber in the Le Mat he adjusted the hammer and spat shot at the back of a fleeing Kansan, hurling him to the snow and staining it. He reloaded on the canter, wheeled, and charged again, snapping at everything that moved on foot. But the camp now was an overturned hornets' nest and he could not separate friend from foe in the confusion of galloping horses and running men. He held his fire until things settled.

They did quite abruptly, the last report crackling away into a distance clad in night and snow. Silence rolled down and landed with a mute thud. The smoke on the field of battle stirred itself groggily and slid sideways to uncover figures spreadeagled on a white ground as in a child's drawing. Among them, clustered and scattered, stood the raiders' horses, their riders wrapped in silence and rapt in their silence. Over it all hung an odor of brimstone.

The peace splintered when a horse started screaming among the mounts picketed on the edge of camp. Several of the animals were down and still. One was struggling to rise, and this was the one making the noise. Its spine was shattered. The Major gestured with his saber and Matthew Stark kneed his horse forward to dispatch the suffering animal. Or maybe it was his brother Israel; Miller could never tell them apart.

After the shot, a horseman came in through the trees to the north, using the horse and a flintlock rifle to shove two men ahead of him on foot. Both were hatless. One had bled down his left leg and was limping. The rider was a man named Simpson, an albino with white hair and pink eyes and skin as pale as plaster, who had been with the militia since November.

"These here near made it away afoot," he reported, reining in before the Major. "I winged the one and the other throwed up his hands."

"You ain't no law!" The uninjured man stood supporting his companion and glaring at the Major. He was gasping and his face glistened. The face was badly pockmarked, with unshorn whiskers sprouting in bunches between and around the craters.

"Hang them for the horse thieves they are," ordered Fouché, and leaned over his pommel to meet the pockmarked man's glare. "When you get to hell and Satan asks why you are there so early, tell him it was for lack of a lookout."

They fought, but Simpson and two of the Starks succeeded at last in binding the condemned men's hands and made nooses of their saddle ropes and slung them around the prisoners' necks and hauled them up from the ground into the upper limbs of the same trees they had tried to escape through, where they kicked for several minutes until their faces turned black and they hung twisting.

The militia had lost two men and a horse. A ball had lodged painfully in Quill's left ham, and Eagle, with a burst of profanity, announced that he had picked up yet another wound, this one in the right calf. One of the raiders then suggested that they cease practicing on lard cans and start using Eagle. The Major, stony-faced in the midst of the answering laughter, looked from the bodies suspended in the trees to those on the ground and gathered his reins. "Our work here is done."

But there was work to do elsewhere, and when word spread of what the militia had done near Independence, many new recruits came to Springfield. By this time there were abolitionists in power in Washington City. As secession fever burned throughout Missouri, more men joined, until the band grew so large the Major was forced to split it into three regiments, taking command of one and promoting Quill and Eagle to captain to head the others. Miller found himself a lieutenant in Eagle's regiment. Kansas invaded Missouri, Missouri invaded Kansas; and 1858 sputtered into 1859, and in April of the election year 1860, Miller celebrated his eighteenth birthday when his regiment drew down on ten Jayhawkers boarding the ferry at Kansas City, lined them up along the south bank, and shot them. The incident reached the eastern newspapers, and although fewer died than in the raid near Independence, the cold premeditation of the act excited much comment and a public condemnation on the floor of Congress.

Kansas was long in answering. The militia was still awaiting retaliation in November, when an unblooded new recruit scarcely older than Miller had been when he shot Curly rode into camp waving a St. Louis newspaper and shouting that Abraham Lincoln had been elected sixteenth President of the United States.

"Let me see it." Turning from the mirror he had tacked to a tree, Major Fouché wiped the remaining lather off his face with a towel and accepted the paper from the excited rider. The others in camp gathered around him. Over his shoulder—or rather past it, for at sixteen he had stopped growing—Miller read of the Missouri legislature's threat to secede in the event Lincoln survived his inauguration.

When the Major lowered the newspaper, his eyes were glittering in their cavernous sockets. "Now," he intoned, "begins the real test."

CHAPTER NINE

Men come in sizes big and small—
in stations low and regal;
The Lord He made them short and tall—
Sam Colt he makes them equal.

On September 1, 1863, in a skirmish with Union regulars in Boone County, Major Charles Fouché took a fragment just above his left knee, but didn't say anything to the surgeon for three days, when he collapsed while attempting to mount his horse. He was moved into a nearby farmhouse, where gangrene was diagnosed and four raiders were pressed to hold him down while the surgeon sawed off the leg. But he did not cut high enough, and by the end of the week it was clear the Major would die.

"I have always held that a man is entitled three great disappointments before his time is through," he told John Miller, himself waiting for a broken arm to knit after a bad fall at Sedalia. It was the only injury he'd suffered in two years of war. "Since I have had but two, I cannot help the conviction that my death is untimely."

He was sitting up in bed with a pillow bunched behind his back and the bandaged stump propped up on another. His words were slurred and his face was flushed, but not from fever. After much protesting he had finally consented to a liberal internal application of liquor to ease the pain.

Miller, seated on the floor of the bedroom with his back to the wall, feeling the vibrations of federal artillery pounding twenty miles to the south, thought he knew which two disappointments the Major was talking about. The first had been the decision on the part of Missouri voters to remain in the Union, the second Richmond's refusal to grant him a commission in the Confederate Army. He had thereupon raised his rank in the militia to colonel while making majors of Eagle and Quill and elevating Miller to captain. But to the raiders he remained the Major.

"What's the third?" Miller asked.

Fouché smiled behind his moustaches, a sure sign of his inebriation. "To see his grandchildren fail."

Such moments of lucidity deserted him soon afterward, and he spent his semiconscious episodes reciting precedents for his professors at Harvard and arguing with his mother about money. Money was of as much concern to Miller, for whom the Major was already dead—as useless as the Le Mat had proven to be beyond a certain range, after which he had traded it for a Navy from a comrade who admired the revolver. At the start of the war, the Major's mother had stopped sending him money, or U.S. marshals had begun seizing it, forcing the militia to place punishing Yankee sympathizers second behind commandeering gold and Treasury greenbacks. Since both were scarce, the Major had stopped paying wages, using the money to feed his troops instead. Desertions had then become a problem for the first time, and between those and their dead (Miller had just that week been obliged to scrape Sergeant Simpson's brains off his pants leg after a ball from a Springfield rifle shattered the albino's skull), the raiders were at their lowest strength since Independence. For some time, only the fervor of Fouché's patriotism had saved them from common banditry; now, with the Major raving out his last hours and the militia's support dwindling among those natives not yet forced out of their homes by General Thomas Ewing's infamous Order No. 11, the war itself seemed little more than a bloody smokescreen for rape and plunder.

When the Major did die, on a wet dawn in the middle of quoting Oliver Wendell Holmes, Miller packed his possessions—mostly dried food and ammunition—into a captured army knapsack, slung it over his right shoulder with a canteen, and left the house. He wore the Navy in a flap holster—more war booty—with the flap cut off for easy access, and his right arm was in a sling fashioned from a farmhouse curtain.

A sentry called for him to halt.

The challenger was just a skinny shadow in the dense ground fog, but Miller recognized his voice. He was the boy who had announced the election of President Lincoln three years before.

"It's me. Miller."

"Oh." Eyes peered through the mist. Not a boy's eyes now. A rifle came down. "How's the Major?"

"Dead."

The sentry went stiff. "Not the Major."

"Go in and see for yourself."

Pause. "Well, where you headed?"

"Out."

"Cap'n Eagle's back the other way." No one but the Major had ever addressed Quill and Eagle by their new rank.

"So's the war. That's how come I'm headed this way."

For a moment the roll of the fog was audible. The rifle came up. "You filthy deserter!"

"Look around," Miller said. "There ain't nothing left to desert."

"Cap'n Quill might not agree. I know you and Eagle are friends. That's why we're going to see Quill. Get them hands up."

He raised his left. "Right's busted."

The eyes that were no longer a boy's moved a little in their sockets. Then, keeping the rifle on his prisoner, the sentry reached out to slide the Navy from Miller's holster. Miller fired his father's Colt's Paterson through the sling.

The sentry's eyes went round, young again. Looking into them, Miller fired a second time. Then he stepped back to let the body fall forward onto its face.

There was shouting in the fog. Someone said, "Yanks!" Gripping the Paterson, Miller half ran around the dead boy and almost collided with one of Quill's men, fat, with a black smudge of beard and a Confederate forage cap down over his eyes. He recognized Miller. "What?"

"I just shot Sergeant Crowder for desertion."

"The hell you say. He's as fired up as the Major."

"Well, take a look." Miller gestured back over his shoulder. When the other raider shifted his eyes, he squeezed the Paterson's trigger. It misfired. Without pausing he crossdrew the Navy with his left hand and laid the barrel hard alongside the man's skull. He grunted and reeled. Miller shoved him aside and ran for the horses.

The camp was alive now, men's raised voices carrying eerily on the fog. A ball whistled close by as Miller yanked loose his roan's tether, mounting on the second try; his splinted arm was getting in his way. Instead of riding out of camp, he spun the horse and galloped back the way he had come, piling over the man from Quill's regiment as he was aiming his revolver again. He went down and the horse leaped over him. Miller whipped the reins across its withers. Shadows swelled out of the fog, only to scramble clear of the path before they too were run down. More shots rang out, but by then he had made the trees on the edge of camp and was in full gallop through the thick gray mists that hung above the ground like smoke over a battlefield.

His plan, once he had placed the camp far enough behind him, was to head southwest, bypassing the Union stronghold at Sedalia and the scene of his disastrous spill, and cross into the Nations. From there westward to the Pacific there was no war. For him it was over, merely writhing out its final days in a delirium of fever and alcohol like the Major's. From Missouri southward the whole country was flushed and raving. The gangrene had spread too far to stop.

His route took him across the one he and Isham Eagle had taken down from the north nine years before. He didn't recognize it. The lush forests he remembered had been burned over in the first year of the war, blasted by Frémont and Lyon into bare scorched earth and stripped trees clawing tormented fingers at a sky made colorless by spent powder. Those houses and barns the mortars had missed yawned empty and orphaned, abandoned at the order of General Ewing in the aftermath of Quantrill's raid on Lawrence the month before; those residents who could not prove loyalty to the Union had been evicted at gunpoint by federal troops. Missouri was conquered land. Miller wondered that he had not seen that earlier, and decided that he had been under a spell, broken at last by the Major's death.

The sun ascended, dragging the fog up with it until it burned off at treetop level. Without thinking, as if he had suddenly been transported back to that furtive journey from the site of Curly's death in 1854, he sought cover to rest and wait for dark. The hills crawled with Yankee patrols looking for guerrillas. In a hollow overhung with thick brush, untouched by battle, he lay listening to the roan graze and working the fingers on the end of his broken arm. Sleep came in patches. Since the morning he had awakened to find Eagle covering him from horseback he had not willingly surrendered himself to un-consciousness.

When night fell he led the roan out of the hollow straight into a patrol of Union infantry.

The moon glimmered through holes in the overcast, shadows of clouds skidding over the semicircle of frozen men in dark uniforms, the muzzles of their Springfields converged like spokes in a broken wheel on the newcomer. Their eyes were lionlike in blank faces. The men with whom Miller had been riding all had eyes and faces just like them. He kept his hand on the roan's bit chain and did not move.

"Who goes there?" demanded a man standing off to the side. He wore a broad-brimmed campaign hat and lieutenant's insignia on his shoulders. He was holding a revolver and looked not much older than Miller.

The ex-militiaman thought swiftly. "Private Morner. Sir."

"What regiment?"

He hesitated. "Eleventh Iowa."

"The Eleventh Iowa. What company?"

"The third."

"Disarm him, Sergeant."

One of the infantrymen lowered his rifle and stepped forward, scooping the Navy Colt out of Miller's holster. Belting it, he patted the prisoner down one-handed, found the other revolver in his sling, and removed that. The sergeant was even younger than his superior; more boy than man. But his movements were sure. He took the bit chain from Miller, and with it his horse.

"There are no Iowa troops in this part of Missouri," the lieutenant informed his prisoner. "And in *this* army, companies are lettered, not numbered. Take him."

Two more soldiers moved in and seized Miller's arms. He bit back a shriek as pain flamed in the one that was broken. The lieutenant took two steps forward and looked down at him. He was two inches taller.

"We haven't the ammunition to waste on rebel spies," he said. "Therefore we shall hang you."

"I ain't no spy."

The hand holding the side arm flashed up. Miller's head exploded.

"Perhaps you like blue."

Miller's eyesight came spinning back, reassembling the lieutenant's face, which had seemed to fly apart when the barrel of the gun met his own temple. Like the rest of the Major's men, and indeed the bulk of the Confederate Army, Miller was wearing mostly Union castoff. His shirt had a hole over the heart, put there by himself shortly before it changed hands.

"Sir, the captain said he wants to interrogate all prisoners." This from one of the other men in the patrol.

"Spies know nothing useful. They are paid to bring back information." The lieutenant was still looking at Miller. He held his gun by the barrel now, ready to use as a bludgeon again. He moved and Miller flinched. But he was merely turning his back on the prisoner. "Bring him. If he falls, drag him until he rises. If he does not rise, cut his throat."

The patrol split into two ranks with Miller in the middle and the sergeant bringing up the rear leading the blue roan. A bayonet jabbed Miller's right kidney and he stumbled forward. His head and arm throbbed, not in rhythm.

It was a long walk in the dark across broken country. The prisoner thought they were looking for an unblasted stand of trees, and he was haunted by the image of two Jayhawkers wriggling like fresh-caught fish at the end of ropes and then just hanging, drifting around lazily in a slight breeze.

But at length he smelled wood smoke, and then they came over a rise that sloped down to where a number of small fires fluttered, flaring occasionally and throwing light over dirty gray canvas and figures moving around in front of them. A sentry challenged the party. The lieutenant gave him a password and they were allowed to enter the camp.

"Hold him here," said the lieutenant, drawing aside the flap of a tent with moth or bullet holes grouped to the right of the sagging peak. "Shoot him if he breaks."

The sergeant led away the captured mount. After that the wait seemed very long. Miller was aware of the eyes and guns on him, and of the scrutiny of a man standing several yards away with a bare hairy belly hanging over his striped uniform trousers and a tobacco bulge in his jaw, who was stirring something in a kettle over an open fire. When the wind shifted, Miller realized the man was boiling his underwear. Aside from that the prisoner appeared to attract only passing attention from the soldiers in camp. The war was two years old and the enemy had lost his novelty.

Finally the tent opened again and a small man in a captain's uniform came out, followed by the lieutenant. The senior officer was twice as old as the oldest man in the patrol, with gray in his stubbly beard and pink scalp glistening through his thinning dark hair. But it wasn't his age that surprised Miller.

"Eugene?" said Ben Honey, his light-colored eyes widening slightly.

CHAPTER TEN

Satan's issue with a gun,
a stranger he to fear;
A blooded wolf at twenty-one,
one dead for every year.

The lieutenant broke the surface of the long silence. "Does the captain know this man?"

"I knew a boy," said Honey; and looked the prisoner over in the light spilling through the tent's open flap. "You have grown some, though not nearly enough."

Miller said nothing. Honey had not grown at all, and seemed smaller than he remembered. But then they had been the same height when Miller was twelve. Honey glanced at the young officer.

"Thank you, Lieutenant. I will interrogate this prisoner in private."

"Sir, the regulations are clear on the treatment of spies."

"They are equally clear on the penalty for insubordination."

There had been no change in Honey's tone. But the short pause that followed the statement crackled. The junior officer saluted. Honey returned the salute and held the flap for Miller to enter the tent. Dismissing the patrol, he went inside behind the prisoner.

"He is right, you know," Honey said. "A rebel captured in Union issue may be hanged or shot for a spy. The rebels pay our informants in the same coin. It is as if this necessary and most dangerous of assignments is uniformly repugnant to both sides." His mouth was wry.

"I ain't in the Confederate Army." Miller stood next to the center pole. Unlike many who were forced to live and do business in tents, neither he nor the captain had to stoop to avoid brushing canvas. This one contained a cot, a folding stool, and a writing table supporting a coal-oil lamp and a map of western Missouri. A bottle of whiskey and a large glass performed as paperweights.

"According to Aristotle one cannot prove a negative." Honey indicated the stool, which Miller at first declined, then accepted. He did refuse whiskey when it was offered. Honey shrugged and splashed liquor into the glass for himself. "In any case, the distinction between a rebel and those who merely support secession is as gray as the uniform. For Lieutenant Danbury it does not exist at all. He would hang a dog if it were named Jefferson Davis."

The captain remained standing, fingering the glass. Miller realized then that he should not have accepted the invitation to sit after all. Honey was now looking down at him. Miller said, "He don't think much better of you."

"He is a career man, and has never forgiven me my past in the Iowa militia. I was called up at the beginning of the war. If it lasts long enough, I may yet attain the rank I held at the end of the fighting in Mexico. I was the youngest lieutenant colonel in that conflict." He drank. "You have gone back to the name Morner?"

"It's the first one that came to me when I was stopped. I'm used to Miller now."

"But for that name I might not have connected you with the John Miller whose letter I carried to your mother through George Sharon. When I saw you I still was not certain. The moustache changes you."

"How *is* Mr. Sharon?"

"Dead. Mormons struck his train bearing supplies to Utah to fight Brigham Young. He never got over the Nebraskans selecting Omaha as their state capital." He hurried on. "Miller is so common that I confess I never thought of you when reports reached me of the young man riding with Charley Slaughter's butchers. If Lieutenant Danbury suspected you were that Miller, he would have ordered you torn to pieces. His men would have done it, too. This war has spawned a new breed of human animal."

"How is my mother?"

"She was well when I left Waterloo, or that was my understanding. We do not speak."

"She hates you." Miller would not ask the question, and Honey would not be drawn out.

"She hates me," Honey agreed.

"She told me you don't have a soul."

"If that is true, I am not alone in this army. Or in this tent," he added. He drained his glass.

"You've got no pulpit to preach from."

The light eyes regarded him. "War made me what I am. You were what you are when this war came. That is my pulpit, should I care to preach. But this conflict is far from over and the words would only catch in my throat." He paused. "Your sister is dead."

He had his reply to Honey's argument all ready; it was a minute before he could take in this last information. Thus his response was inane. "What?"

"They buried her shortly before I left. She was stricken with scarlatina the first winter you were away."

"She recovered! My mother wrote—"

"What a mother writes and what is true are continents apart. She was afraid that if you knew your sister was ill you would rush home, where you would be arrested for murder, or more probably lynched. The sickness weakened her, made her prey to every miasma that came along. People were surprised she lived as long as she did."

"You're lying!" But he held his seat. He thought of grave, pretty eyes in a child's face.

Honey's own were curiously sad.

"Two years ago," he said, "I might have felt compelled to call you out for terming me a liar. As you get older the insult does not seem so bad, possibly because you know in your heart it is true. And then again perhaps this is not unique to age, or to me. When all this killing is done I fear we will none of us be what we were."

He was pouring himself another drink when young Lieutenant Danbury reentered the tent and snapped to attention. He didn't look at Miller.

"Sir, Sparks reports the telegraph to St. Louis is operating."

"We can expect a respite, then. General Grant only cuts the wires before a campaign, to avoid interference from Washington City."

"Will that be all, sir?"

"Have someone escort our prisoner to the stockade. I have dispatches to get out now that the wires are up."

Danbury's eyes flickered between Miller and the captain, hatred battling confusion. "The stockade, sir?"

"Yes. It would not do for him to hang before I am through with my interrogation."

The "stockade" was not that at all, but rather a quarter-acre pit into which two dozen Confederate and near-Confederate prisoners had been deposited, and no more than six feet deep at its lowest. A healthy man would have no trouble scrambling out, only to pitch back in clobbered with holes from the rifles of the sentries that patrolled the edges day and night. By day the occupants, wearing the rags of their old uniforms mixed with mufti and Union blue, wandered the confines or sat with their backs to the earthen walls and talked of home. One youth, towheaded and barefoot and seventeen at the outside, had a scar on his right cheek that had been stitched poorly, drawing the corner of his mouth into a smirk and exposing two black teeth.

"Pea Ridge," he boasted, when Miller asked about the wound. "Was a bone from my sarge's leg done it. He got hit by a mortar shell and a piece of it flied up and catched me. Where was yourn?"

Miller rubbed his arm, which ached fiercely from its recent hard use. "Sedalia."

"Them Yanks hold a grudge till it hollers mammy."

They relieved themselves into buckets attached to ropes that were then hauled up and dumped into the latrine by other prisoners who had taken the oath of loyalty to the Union. Sometimes the buckets stood forgotten or neglected for days. The stink grew as thick as soup and studded with flies. At night the earth smell was even worse, moldy and dank. Miller stayed awake nights and slept during the day to avoid the sensation of sleeping in a grave. It only reminded him of Maureen.

He kept track of the days in his head the first week; after that he scraped notches in his wooden splint with the edge of a thumbnail. He was scraping a third when a sentry called from the edge of the pit. "Morner!"

They let him make his own way up, which was more difficult than he had expected. Like the rest he had been fed thin soup and sometimes a square of bread dried hard as a tree root, and with his injured arm it was barely enough to sustain the effort. He knew then why there had been no escapes during his stay. The only way out of that pit short of swearing the oath was to starve.

He was greeted in the captain's tent by Ben Honey, who looked up from his writing table and said, "Prison life appears not to have done you lasting harm. You looked rather too well fed when you arrived. Chicken-stealing is a capital offense in this army."

"Then I reckon there's a dead man for every wing bone I seen in camp," said Miller.

"The commander cannot be everywhere." He lifted a yellow flimsy from the table. "I have received orders to move this unit south. The fighting is over in Missouri and we will be rejoining the war any day now."

"Prisoners going along, or you fixing to shoot them right here?"

The sentry who had brought him cuffed the back of his head hard. "Quit interrupting the captain."

"Thank you, Corporal. Wait outside." When the sentry was gone: "Execution has been suggested, and if I were to open the matter to voting I hold no illusions that Christian good fellowship will prevail. The majority of these troops hails from Kansas. However, the Army being an autocracy; I have made arrangements instead to ship the bulk of the captured rebels back east to the federal prison at Elmira."

"What about the rest?"

"Those adjudged spies will be dealt with in the manner prescribed by military law."

"Shot."

"Shot," he confirmed, "or hanged."

Miller's face felt icy. But he said: "Well, do 'er, then."

"One might expect a dedicated fighter like yourself to show more concern for your compatriots." Honey's brows were raised—exaggeratedly, Miller thought.

"Compatriots?" Honey's schoolboy English puzzled him as thoroughly at twenty-one as it had at twelve.

"I have two documents before me." The captain slid aside the flimsy and raised another sheet from the table. "The first is a pass that will take you out of this camp and past any Union troops you may encounter in this sector. It awaits only my signature."

"The other?" He had not intended to ask the question Honey was so plainly taunting. But it had come out anyway.

"The other"—he turned another sheet so that it faced the prisoner—"awaits yours."

He didn't look at it. "The oath."

"Good men have signed it before this. Some better than you."

"I seen them, pulling up buckets of shit."

"What I am offering amounts to a full amnesty. If you refuse to sign I can have you removed from this tent and executed immediately. Hanged, I should think, since you seem to fear that most." He dipped a horsehair pen into the table's built-in ink vessel and held it out.

"I reckon it's the rope for me then," said Miller.

Honey sat back, bending the pen thoughtfully between hard small hands.

"Does no man's death move you," he said, "not even your own?"

"Hang me and be damned."

Wonder flickered in the captain's light eyes—and died. He stirred, slid the first sheet over the unsigned oath, and scribbled his signature at the bottom. He rocked a blotter over it and extended the paper folded. "I think that I have held you here this long because I haven't a likeness of myself at your age."

Miller hesitated, then took the paper and unfolded and read it. It was what he had said it was.

"This is the second time I have delivered you against my own best interests and better judgment," Honey said. "Next time I fear you will find my stores of generosity quite plundered."

"What about my guns?"

Honey stared. Then he busied himself redipping his pen. "Will you be returning home to your mother and brothers?"

"They've got along without me this long."

"Then the guns will remain government property, as they would have had you signed the oath. I am not in the business of rearming enemies of my country."

"My horse, then."

Honey continued writing without looking up. "You forget. One horse is exactly what you owe me."

They spoke no more, and Miller walked out of the tent breathing air not tainted by dirt and human waste.

CHAPTER ELEVEN

A man said it once, I can't say just who,
it meets everywhere with a nod;
No law will you find to the west of St. Lou,
and west of Missouri, no God.

Emporia, Kansas, December 1865.

The unheated hallway on the second floor of Mme. Phillipe's Hospitality House smelled of damp plaster, the worn burgundy runner crosshatched with slushy bootprints. Pausing before the first door off the landing, the newcomer to town eased a long-barreled Remington revolver out of the belt holster at his groin, caught his breath to prevent vapor, and threw a heel at the lock. The latch broke and the door swung all the way around on its hinges, slamming the inside wall with a noise like a shotgun blast. He entered the room in two leaps and took hold of the naked man kneeling on the bed by his hair and bent him backward, inserting the muzzle under his chin.

"Bill Broadhead?" he demanded.

"Wha—Broadhead? Jesus, my back!" Befuddled and sweat-smelling, the man was bowed almost double. Moonlight coming through the window fell flatly on the face of the naked woman under him, a black hole of screaming mouth in a mask of white powder streaked with sweat.

Miller ignored her. Letting go of the man's hair, he curled his gun arm around his throat instead and used the free hand to pull a Wanted reader out of his pocket and snap it open, comparing the steel engraving with the frightened features. "Your pardon," he said, releasing him. He touched his hat to the screaming woman and let himself out into the hallway.

The man in the next room had heard the noise. When his door

flew open he greeted Miller standing, his gun belt over one bare shoulder and a Starr double-action revolver in his left hand. Both guns went off at the same instant. A red blossom opened high on the naked torso, glistening in the chest hairs, and he took one step back before falling forward onto his face.

Miller opened his buffalo coat to look at the two holes where the dead man's bullet had transfixed the hide, missing his ribs by less than an inch. He strode inside to lift the man's face, let it drop with a thud, and turned to the woman in the bed. This one was a mop of rust-colored hair and two huge eyes above the sheet she had drawn up over herself.

"Who was he?" he demanded.

The reply was delayed and came filtered through the sheet. "Don't you know?"

"His nose ain't big enough to be Bill Broadhead's."

"I don't know his name," she said. "I'm new."

"Shit."

He holstered the weapon and struck a match. The woman shrank toward the flocked wall, but he turned his back on her, lifted the glass chimney off the lamp on the bedstand, and lit the wick. In the yellow light he dug a sheaf of travel-worn circulars out of a pouch inside the buffalo coat and got down on one knee to check the dead man's features against the engravings and descriptions.

"Get up slow, mister."

He didn't obey immediately. He finished reading the document in front of him and slid it behind the last sheet in the stack. Then he rose, keeping both hands in plain sight.

"Turn around."

He complied. A big man filled the doorway. He was six inches taller than Sam Woodlawn and fully as wide, one shoulder inside the room, the other hidden by the doorframe. His bare head was large and bald and his muttonchop whiskers were as dark as lampblack. He had suspenders on over a striped shirt without a collar and no coat. His weapon was a shotgun cut back almost to the stock, held in both hands, its twin barrels big enough to spray the room.

"Man pulled down on me," Miller said. "The whore'll tell you it was self-defense."

"Keep your hands where I can see 'em," said the other. "No, let the belt be. You get near that there gun they'll be scraping you off the wall with a razor. What's your name, mister?"

"John Miller."

"What's your business?"

"I heard a man named Bill Broadhead was in Emporia, paying attention to the girls at Madam Phillip's." Like everyone else who carried away the name of the disorderly house, he Anglicized it. "He's wanted for desertion under fire. Army's paying a reward for him dead or alive."

"Bounty killer."

"No, sir. I just hunt down cowards and traitors. It's my patriotic duty."

The big man's eyes were Indian black in the lamplight, motionless and dead of expression. "I heard tell of a John Miller was riding with them Missouri border killers during the war," he said. "He wasn't such a much of a patriot in them days. I also hear tell the Army's the only one around with money to put up rewards."

"Who are you?"

"I had time to put my coat on next door when you kilt this man, you'd see the star. I'm marshal here." He twitched the shotgun toward the corpse. "He Broadhead?"

"No. I reckon Broadhead wasn't here or else he let himself out a window when he heard me coming. But this one serves the reader on Chester LaPlante, another deserter on the list. I got it right here." He waved the circulars.

"Get it and read it to me." This to the prostitute in the bed, who lowered the sheet to smirk.

"I could read, you think I'd work here?"

"Toss them over," he told Miller. "So's I can count the hairs on the back of your wrist while you're at it. I miss one you're stew meat."

Keeping his right hand raised, Miller stooped and flipped the papers so that they landed at the marshal's feet without scattering. The other waited until he straightened before crouching to lift them, eyes and shotgun on Miller. They were watching each other through a fog of smoke still swirling from the exchange of gunfire minutes before.

A crowd of men and women in several stages of dress had gathered in the hallway outside. One, a very tall woman corseted into a perfect hourglass, hair dyed bright orange, stepped forward. "He said his name was Sherman," she reported.

"General?"

She met Miller's grin with the cold gaze of a proprietress. "I did not ask him his rank."

"See can you find Chester LaPlante." The marshal passed the papers back over his shoulder.

She paged through them swiftly, wetting her thumb like a banker counting greenbacks. "Yes." She read it and looked up. "Why, this description does not fit Mr. Sherman at all."

Miller said, "He's got him a scar on his chin."

"It is more on his lip. And he was fair, not dark as it says here."

"Well, Mr. Miller, it appears you're just a common killer," said the marshal, and for the first time white teeth flashed behind his whiskers. "I bet you didn't guess I was a poet. Neither did I, till just now. Madam Phillip, if you'll collect Mr. Miller's iron for me we'll go ahead and remove ourselves from your place of business."

She hesitated. "What about Mr. Sherman?"

"Oh, Jubal Lansdale will oblige you there. He ain't buried anyone this month."

Miller allowed the woman to relieve him of his Remington. He had entertained the prospect of seizing and using her as a shield, but the closer she got the bigger she looked, until she was towering over him. She smelled thickly of scent. The marshal accepted the weapon from her and thrust it under the waistband of his trousers.

"He wasn't wanted," Miller said, "how come he tried gunning me?"

"I'm thinking he don't favor receiving visitors with guns in just his skin. 'Course, that's only a guess." The marshal stepped aside, gesturing with the shotgun. "You first, Mr. Killer Miller."

The jail was next door. They walked over boards gone iron-hard from the cold and through a door into a room made stifling by a barrel stove glowing in one corner. Another door led to the cells in back, where the marshal kicked the bars, rousing a fat man from a cot inside one of the cells.

The man was as tall as the marshal, and as broad across the middle as the marshal was across the shoulders, tapering down to small feet in dirty socks and up to a head of bowl-cut brown hair and shaggy jowls that shifted like saddlebags as he drew his suspenders up over sloping shoulders. His eyes were small and sharp like raisins in raised bread and a brass star shone on his underwear top. "Yes, Mr. Stonewarden," he said, blinking.

"Frank, Mr. Miller here's staying with us till the judge decides how high to hang him. I got to give him your bed on account of I can hear what goes on inside this cell from the office."

"Yes, sir." The fat man rolled up his bedding, lifted a pair of cracked boots from the floor, and stepped out through the open cell door, looking at Miller curiously. He stank.

"Inside." Marshal Stonewarden held the door for the prisoner, who obeyed. It shut with a clatter and the marshal turned the key in the lock and pulled it out. He looked at Miller through the bars.

"Frank will be sleeping in the cell next door," he said. "He's got him a horse pistol in one of them boots and so far he's used it on two prisoners trying to escape. One's dead, the other might as well be. Frank is simpleminded. He don't understand it's wrong to kill folks and I just never got around to setting him straight."

"Killers don't scare me."

"Mister, I don't give antelope shit what scares you. I'm only being Christian and telling you what will happen you go to thinking there's any way out of here but thirteen steps to a short drop. What you do with the information is betwixt you and whoever it is lowdown murdering Missouri trash says its prayers to."

He went out, leaving open the door to the office. Frank, standing in the narrow passageway with his boots in one hand and his bedding rolled up under his other arm, stared at Miller a while longer before going into the next cell. There he made his bed and lowered himself onto it with a drawn-out grunt, like a bear preparing to hibernate. He slept facing Miller's cell with his back to the wall and one hand inside one of his boots. His snoring set the bars rattling.

Miller stretched out on his own cot, bare canvas now, the slats striping his back. He didn't sleep. In two years he had come full circle and was a prisoner again. He had spent part of that time working for Indians in the Nations, chopping wood and fetching water for members of the so-called Five Civilized Tribes while the war glutted out its final months like some crazed wounded animal devouring its own spilled vitals; and learned that a white man forced to serve Indians was lower than the most miserable black slave. He had labored sixteen hours a day for food that made him long for the Union's hard bread and watery soup, slept on cornshuck mattresses in hay cribs whose slats let in the pounding summer sun and blowing winter snow, had been tested and humiliated by illiterate savages delighted with the white man in their debt. But with the war's end he had sunk the axe so deep in the block that Old Abe himself couldn't have loosened it, and gone drifting.

About that time posters had begun to appear promising cash for federal deserters brought in alive or dead. Several of the descriptions and engravings had seemed to match men he had seen in his travels, and while a newly spliced nation was mourning and celebrating the death of its first murdered President and getting the straight of the new man in the White House, John Miller had entered Fort Scott leading two horses with a dead man slung across each saddle and come away with four hundred dollars for their delivery. Like many others, he had looked at Reconstruction and seen nothing but opportunities for a man with the proper skills.

In contemplation of this happy vision he dozed, to awaken in morning light and look at Marshal Stonewarden unlocking the door to his cell. At the noise, Frank sprang to his feet with a speed incredible for one of his bulk, in his hand a Colt's Dragoon big enough to bring the rest of him into normal perspective. His tiny eyes glittered.

"Frank, it's me."

It was a command. For a space the mountainous deputy held his ground, like a dog with its hackles standing. Then the glitter went out of his eyes and he returned the big revolver to the boot in his other hand.

"The town know about him?" asked Miller, rising.

"Oh, he was town pet before I taken him on here. We all got up money to buy him a substitute when the Army drafted him in '62. He took to this work real good. Some claim too good, but them that claim that ain't marshal." He swung open the door and stood away from the opening.

Miller didn't move. He glanced down at the marshal's hands, empty of the shotgun for the first time since they had met.

"You waiting for breakfast or what?" said Stonewarden. "Step out."

"I step out, Frank shoots me for running; that it?"

"Frank, put down the boot." The deputy obeyed. "I got to chewing on how ready that dead one was to put you under when you walked in on him, and then I dug out that last batch of circulars that came Monday. Looking for that scarred lip. Then I went over to Lansdale's Mortuary for my first real gape. His name's Gunderson and he's wanted in Arkansas for stabbing a nigger. Carpetbaggers want him sore bad."

"How sore?"

"Alive, five hunnert. Dead, three. You damaged the goods there some. Anyways, I wired Topeka, and you ain't wanted just now so I'm cleaning out the barn. Find your best road out of town and stay on it."

"What about the three hundred for Gunderson?"

Stonewarden's face set. He had on a brown slouch hat, and with his bald head covered he looked ten years younger, a tired thirty. His collarless neck was raw from shaving and the star on his rumpled coat wanted polish, unlike Frank's, which shone like a fresh penny.

"Town council pays me fifty a month and a quarter for every rat and stray dog I shoot inside the limits," he said. "I got a wife that likes nice things and there ain't enough dogs and rats in town to keep a smile on her face. Sometimes I got to go outside and shoot them and drag them back over the line. You think on that on your way down the road and I bet it comes to you what about that three hundred."

Miller put on his hat and buffalo coat and accompanied the marshal into the office, where his Remington was returned to him. He inspected the cylinder.

Stonewarden said, "I taken out the cartridges. Your horse is over at Carson's Livery. You owe Carson fifty cents."

"How much of that gets back to you?"

"Pleasure having you, Mr. Miller. Don't come back."

He was riding a chestnut with a white blaze that year, eighteen hands high and broken to gunfire, so that a rider could knock the heads off prairie dogs at full gallop and never miss a one. He had bought it from a breeder in Fort Scott out of the reward for his first two deserters. After leaving Emporia he turned its head north in the direction of Junction City, where rumor said a former cavalry lieutenant had fled with the company payroll.

Snow blanketed the flat country, with rivers running black through it and gusty winds combing the grains into heaps around trees and against hills. He rode with his collar standing and the brim of his hat tilted down to his nose, but the razor winds found his neck and sliced up under his sleeves and pants legs. His fingers grew stiff inside their thin leather gloves. At sundown he camped on the lee side of what passed for a hill in Kansas and warmed them carefully over a small fire before getting out his foodstuffs. He had long since learned to tend them as lovingly as he did his guns.

Later, his belly full of salt pork, he poured a second cup of coffee and set the pot back on its flat rock next to the fire. A horse blew then, the sound snatched away on the wind. Moving just his eyes, he looked at his own mount browsing in the snow, downwind and out of earshot. Without pausing or changing his pace he transferred the cup from right hand to left and rose, stretching himself and turning his back in the direction from which the noise had come. When he came around the rest of the way, the Remington was in his hand. He cocked it.

The two horsemen drew rein at twenty feet. One was tall and thin and wore a soft black hat with a narrow brim, the other short and round with a pearl gray derby screwed down to his eyes. A luxuriant growth of black beard grew past his neck into his coat like an ascot, the hairs around his mouth standing out stiff and white. His partner was clean-shaven and his ears stuck out. Both had on town coats that were plainly unequal to the prairie cold.

"Sir, we come in peace."

The bearded man's voice was astonishingly deep. Miller trained the revolver between the pair, ready to move in either direction. "Who does?"

"My business partner, Daniel J. Black." The bearded man indicated his companion. "I am Howard Rippert. Perhaps on your way through Emporia you espied a sign reading RIPPERT AND BLACK CART-AGE COMPANY. That is ours. We are also president and vice president of the Emporia Businessmen's Alliance."

"If you're looking to join me up you have the wrong man."

"If you will allow us five minutes by your fire we shall explain ourselves. I think I speak for Mr. Black as well as for myself when I confess that we are not as well equipped as you for this climate."

"Throw down your guns and we'll talk about it."

"Sir, we are unarmed. May I?" He touched one of the buttons on his coat.

Miller nodded, watching him closely. Rippert unbuttoned the coat and carefully drew it open. At his signal, Black did the same. There were no arms in sight. Miller told them to step down but kept his gun steady.

They led their mounts into the firelight and tethered them to a clump of sumac. Afoot they made a comical pair, Black long and cadaverous, Rippert plump and shorter than Miller. They spread their coats in front of the fire and turned around and lifted the tails to warm their backsides. Miller holstered the Remington.

Rippert said, "You are not an easy man to follow, Mr. Miller. Had we started ten minutes later the wind would have obliterated your tracks entirely."

"What's your business here, Mr. Rippert?"

"Toward the end we were forced to follow the tantalizing aroma of your coffee."

Miller handed him his own cup. "Only one I got."

"You are a Christian, sir." He drank, warming both hands around the steaming tin.

"You know my name."

Rippert made a noise, swallowed, and released one hand to reach inside his coat. Miller touched his gun. But the bearded man drew out only a folded newspaper, which he handed to his host. "Third column, sir. You are better known than you think."

It was that day's Emporia *Bulletin*. Miller unfolded it, turned it toward the fire, and read the stacked headlines.

A SHOOTING IN OUR CITY
DESPERADO KILLED DEBAUCHING IN HOUSE OF DOUBTFUL FAME
"FAIR FIGHT," REPORTS WOMAN WHO WITNESSED IT
BORDER HERO DISPATCHES TRAITOR
AVENGER'S GUN LIKE LIGHTNING
"KILLER" MILLER

The rest of the column was a solid block of gray in the firelight. He refolded the newspaper. "Border hero?"

"The editor is a former proslaver," Rippert explained. "A purple account, I am certain. But all the talk around town is of you. A special meeting of the alliance was called in your benefit; however, it ran long, and by the time Mr. Black and I received our charges you had left."

"I got no charges against me," Miller said quickly.

"No, sir, no; certainly not. I was referring to our mission, Mr. Black's and mine; which is to ask you to place your considerable gifts at the service of Emporia's good citizens."

"There's a point in there somewhere, Mr. Rippert. I wish you'd spit it out."

"We have come, sir, and if it is a nuisance I beg your pardon, and you are of course free to accept or reject the proposal as you will, this being a free Union for which we have gone thrice to war"—he colored—"not, that is to say, that those who fought for the Confederacy did not share this aim—"

"Give it up, Howard," broke in Black. "Mr. Miller, we've been authorized to offer you the post of city marshal. The pay is sixty dollars a month if you're interested."

CHAPTER TWELVE

All wars must end, but death lives on,
the bloody spore spread far;
To quell the conflict's deadly spawn,
John Miller wore a star.

Miller, a veteran of the frontier practice of "greening," although he himself had almost no sense of humor, looked from Rippert to Black for some sign of it in their faces. But the little man's expression was lost in his beard, and his clean-shaven partner's was grave as cut stone. He decided to play the hand he had been dealt.

"You got a marshal now."

"Jack Stonewarden is dependable when it comes to jailing inebriates and shooting stray animals," Rippert conceded. "But of guns he knows next to nothing. He is a former boxer and believes himself capable of resolving most situations with his fists. A gun man like yourself is better equipped to handle the sort of animal that has come slinking through Kansas since the war."

"His scattergun looked plenty capable last night."

"Yes, but he is too often without it."

"I thought the town council appointed the marshal."

"The alliance appoints the city council," said Black.

Miller threw some green sticks on the fire. They popped and spat. Rippert buttoned his coat.

"You will want to sleep on it, naturally," he said, all his unease vanished. "We open our doors tomorrow at eight. If you are interested we will hear your answer then."

"You can have it now. Thanks and no. The bounty business pays better and I'm my own boss."

"Oh, but your office will not stand in the way of any rewards that may come in your direction. Meanwhile you will be on salary, and your room and board are provided. There is talk, too, of a pension."

"That shiny star draws too much fire for sixty and found."

Rippert began an elaborate denial, but Black cut him short. "Perhaps there's a figure we can agree on that will make the risk worthwhile."

"A hundred a month."

"That is twice what we are paying Stonewarden now!" Rippert protested. "The city treasury—a protracted, expensive war—"

Miller said, "Emporia was a cookpot and two log outhouses when the war came along. It got big selling goods to both armies and buying Confederate graybacks for pennies on the dollar and then paying them out in change at face value. A hundred's my price, Mr. Rippert. Naturally you'll want to sleep on it. There's space there by the fire. My doors open at first light. You can give me your answer then."

The bearded man looked to his partner, but Black was watching the gun man. "You'll have your hundred, Mr. Miller. The others will howl, but we're holding notes from half of them and the rest bend with the prevailing wind. Will you ride back to town with us?"

"I'll be in tomorrow. We'll try it for a spell, see does it work out. What's my first job?"

"The same as Stonewarden's when we appointed him: turning your predecessor out of the office." Black slipped his mount's tether and swung a long leg over the saddle. "Emporia is proud to extend its hospitality, Mr. Miller. Try not to wear it out."

Morning was well along when John Miller entered the marshal's office for the second time, this time of his own choosing. He found Stonewarden in his shirtsleeves cleaning out the big oak desk and poking the items into a gunnysack. He didn't look up as his successor approached.

"Rifles and ammunition are locked up in that case yonder," he said. "Key's in the rolltop, second drawer down on the right. New batch of circulars on top. Came in this morning and I didn't get the chance to look through them. You'll want to so's you know which ones to stay away from they come to town."

"You act anxious to get out." Miller tossed his bedroll onto a maple chair.

"I figure to get used to walking on the light side of the street again quick as possible. Damn star's just a mark to shoot at." He took it off his coat on the back of the desk swivel and flipped it at Miller. "There. It put holes in both my shirts."

Miller rubbed it on his coatsleeve to get the green off. "Don't I get sworn in or something?"

"My job when the judge ain't in. I forget the words, but raise your right hand and say 'I do.'"

He did that and pinned it on under his coat. "Where you headed?"

"California gold fields. Send for my wife later. I won't get rich, but I won't get bit by no drunken whores neither. Last time my hand swoll up big as a calf and the doc had to lance it with a knitting needle. I leave you that, and this too." He lifted a fringed rose satin pillow from the swivel and let it fall back. "You'll get the piles soon enough you spend enough time on your ass listening to Aurora Preuss try to talk you into letting her boy Merle loose early to milk the cows. He'll be busy busting up Madam Phillip's Saturday night like always."

"You looked pretty fit over that scattergun the other night, if that's worth anything to you," Miller said.

Stonewarden looked at him for the first time. Scars showed on his bald head where fists had raked its slick surface.

"Don't waste none of it on me, Miller. You're a Missouri murdering son of a bitch in front of that star or behind it, and a hunnert Howard Ripperts and Dan Blacks can't make no lapdog out of a coyote. They'll come to see that for themselves quick enough. But by then I'll be panning gold up in the mountains in the daytime and walloping the whores in San Francisco at night."

"What about Frank?"

"Frank's went home, quit when he heard I got fired. He wanted to come with me to California but I told him I'd have hell enough feeding my ownself without looking to him too. He went out blubbering like a big fat baby. Won't work for no one but me."

"Sorry to hear that. I can use him if he's like you say."

"I tried out two deputies ahead of him and got shut of 'em both. First wouldn't bust a cap on a hornet if it was stinging his eye and the other shot folks for looking at him cross, like you. Town hanged him. But Frank, you can count on him to use that gun on whatever you want a hole in, and not to when you don't. All you got to do is point."

"Would he stay on if you did, do you figure?"

"He would. But I ain't." He closed the last drawer and tied a knot in the top of the sack. "Good luck, Mr. Killer Miller. Or more better, good luck to them that cross your trail. Don't bother looking for me at your hanging."

He put on his coat, lifted the slouch hat off a spindle of telegraph flimsies, and carried the gunnysack toward the door. Miller watched him.

"I'll split my pay with you if you stay on. Fifty and fifty."

Stonewarden stopped and turned his head just enough to show the line of his cheek.

"I figure I can trust you not to backshoot me," Miller explained. "Also I want Frank. He's like an extra gun hand and I can use all of them I can get."

"Town's full of them. Getting fuller by the day since the war."

"I don't know any of them."

"You don't know me."

"I don't," Miller agreed. "But I do."

Stonewarden remained unmoving. "I don't see where it can work out."

"Hell, likely it won't. I told Rippert and Black I'd just try the work on for a time. If it don't fit, one or the both of us can always walk."

"I own a part interest in the Jackrabbit. Told my wife to mail me any offers I got. I stay on, I ain't sharing it."

"I ain't after any saloons you got pieces of. There's plenty more. We can both make ourselves a living and never have to talk to each other except in here."

Stonewarden turned around. "Mr. Miller, that part appeals to me."

"There's just one thing. You hire on here you got to stop calling me things like Killer Miller. Names like that have a way of sticking on you. They draw trouble."

Stonewarden said, "It ain't the name."

Dusk came drifting into the office through the big front windows. It was Miller's most trying time of day: too dark to do anything constructive, not dark enough to spend kerosene. Add to that the jerky whisper of Frank's broom sweeping out the cells in back, and the new marshal's nerves were standing on end. He got up from behind the desk and started pacing. "When's rounds?"

"Six." Stonewarden, seated at the rolltop desk in the corner, had laid aside the wanted circulars and was cracking his big knuckles in order.

"This what it's like every day?"

"No, it quiets down toward the other end of the week."

Something pecked at the door. "What was that?"

"What was what?"

Miller was silent. After a moment the pecking resumed. "That." Drawing the Remington he went to the door and pulled it open.

A big black man in overalls was standing outside. He snatched a filthy cloth cap off a head as bald as Stonewarden's with a coiled gray fringe hooked over his ears and said, " 'Evenin', sir. The marshal, he in?"

"You're talking to him, Canaan," called Stonewarden from behind Miller. "There's been some shaking up done since we talked last. Trouble at the livery?"

"Yessir. Mr. Carson, he's home sick again and he says to me he says, 'Canaan, you're in charge, and don't you come pulling me out of this here sickbed exceptin' it's a real emergency.' Well, I think I got me one, only the last time I got him out of that there sickbed he fired me for a week, and with Rachel in a fambly way and all—"

Miller said, "You want to tell us what's going on while it's still an emergency?"

Canaan rolled his eyes in that way Miller was convinced was entirely an act. "Well, these here two strangers, they's killin' each other over whose is it this here horse belongs to."

"Guns or fists?" Stonewarden was on his feet.

"Knives."

Stonewarden started toward the door, then held up. "You first, Marshal."

"Don't you want to take along the scattergun?"

"It's guns to guns, fists to fists and knives. Unless you hanker doing it different, being the new marshal and all."

Miller paused. "It's your town until it's mine."

The former marshal called Frank in from the back and the three accompanied Canaan outside and across two streets to Carson's Livery.

"I didn't hear Rachel was expecting again," said Stonewarden on the way. "How many does that make?"

"Five, with Gerald gone to join up with the Tenth Cavalry." Canaan's long stride kept taking him ahead of his companions and he had to break step to avoid the lead.

"When you two going to take time out to visit a preacher?"

"Well, she's Presbyterian and I'm Southern Baptist and we can't agree on which one to pick."

The two combatants were on the packed earth floor between the stalls, rolling in the manure and cursing while the horses shied and snorted behind the doors. They both had on heavy overcoats and one had lost his hat. Each man had a knife and was grasping the other's wrist with his free hand. The newcomers watched them for a while. Neither man appeared to hold the advantage for long.

"Even match," said Miller.

"I'd take the one with the whiskers over distance," Stonewarden said. "He's got him a deep chest."

"Where's the horse?" Miller asked Canaan.

"That gray there. I put him back in the stall when the fight started."

"Whose is it really?"

"Don't know. It's one Mr. Carson taken in."

"Well, get Carson and ask him."

"It ain't that simple," Stonewarden told him. "Carson's mooncrazy. Slips his tether oncet every three-four weeks and makes his wife tie him down before he takes to hurting someone. He gets that way he don't know a gray horse from a black walnut."

"He's that bad he ought to be locked up."

"Town needs the livery. You see there, I told you."

The bearded fighter Stonewarden had favored was on top now, his knife hand making progress toward his opponent's throat despite the other's grip on his wrist. Their congested faces were flecked with each other's spittle.

"Trot out the gray," Miller told the black man.

Canaan unlatched the stall and led the horse out by its bridle. It was a small mix with racing lines, an even charcoal color all over. Its eyes were clear and bold.

"Hell, I'd fight for him myself," Stonewarden said.

Miller said, "Frank."

Without hesitation the great shaggy fat man scooped the Colt's Dragoon out of his loose left boot and shot the horse between the eyes. It threw up its head and grunted and its legs splayed out as it went down. Canaan, frozen with shock, barely let go of the bridle in time to avoid being pulled down with it.

"You weren't lying about Frank," Miller told Stonewarden. His voice was deadened in the ringing aftermath of the explosion.

"No, he's a wonder."

At the sound of the shot, the fighters had separated. The deep-chested one with whiskers rose first, followed a second later by his hatless opponent. Straw and manure plastered their coats. They stared open-mouthed at the dead horse lying with its tongue caught between its teeth. The man without a hat remembered his knife then and raised it, glaring at Miller.

"Who the hell are you, killing a good animal like that?"

"Frank."

Frank had replaced the spent cap on the Colt's with a fresh one and pointed the long barrel at the hatless man. Miller said:

"One of you is a thief. I could find out which, but it takes longer than any of you is worth and after it got done you wouldn't neither of you be worth nothing. So I'm going to be bighearted and give you till full dark to hire a horse or a mule or a big yellow dog and find some other town to do your thieving and fighting in. After that I turn Frank here loose."

"Well, what about my rig?" demanded the man with the whiskers.

"*My* rig!" said the other.

"That goes to the livery to settle the bill and haul off the carcass. That sit all right with you, Canaan?"

"Yessir," the black man said.

"Full dark," Miller reminded the others, and turned away.

Walking back to the office, Frank trailing behind, Stonewarden said: "Solomon did a thing like that oncet. Only he didn't really cut the baby in two."

"I hate killing animals," said Miller.

CHAPTER THIRTEEN

> But the lawman's life is a lonely life,
> of friends he numbers none;
> Though his wish may be to take a wife,
> his vows are to his gun.

Her name was Laurel DePaul, although it came out Laurie in *Harper's New Monthly* in December 1879, and when the moving pictures got around to telling John Miller's story twenty-three years after his death they called her Lauren Dawes and made her a schoolteacher—which she was once, in another place two years before Miller met her in Madame Phillipe's Hospitality House in Emporia, Kansas. Some said she'd left a husband and a small child in Dayton before coming West. In October 1952 a man who gave his name as Clarence DePaul Miller, dying of pneumonia in a hospital for the indigent in Chicago, gave an interview to a newspaper in which he claimed to be the illegitimate son of John Miller and Laurel DePaul, born in Emporia in 1867, but as the Lyon County courthouse burned down sixteen years after that no records exist to prove or deny this assertion. Found among his effects was an old locket containing a postage-stamp-size tintype of a young dark-haired woman with wide-set eyes and a small, pointed chin, which, if the old man's story was true, could be the only known existing likeness of the one woman said to have claimed John Miller's heart. She was twenty-three when they met in May 1866.

She had hair that looked blue-black by lamplight but showed glints of red in summer sunshine, or it did in that first year of their acquaintance. When they met again in Wyoming in 1873 it was starting to glitter with steel shavings, and by Dakota 1880 it was black again—a harsh, flat black that brought out the lines in her face. The reason for the confusion over her name had to do with the failure of a New York journalist named Frazee to get Laurel to collaborate on a book about the life of John Miller, then dead ten days; costing her a place in legend. The 1903 moving picture used this and explained how in a fit of grief and rage she turned the man out of her house at gunpoint. In reality she had demanded too much money for her cooperation and Frazee went ahead and wrote the book without her and without mentioning her.

Whether she loved him, or whether he just represented customer reliability in a time and place that cared nothing for the requirements of a woman alone, is lost to history. But over a period of fourteen years, in locations a thousand miles apart, she remains the only woman whom documents can place at three key points in John Miller's short life.

Jack Stonewarden's diary, published posthumously in 1910, identifies her at the scene when Miller learned of the robbery of the Farmer's Trust in Emporia, one day short of six months after the former marshal swore in his successor.

"By *daylight?*" Throwing aside the coverlet in the room across the hall from the one in which he had killed Gunderson, Miller ignored his underwear and pulled a shirt and trousers on over a body that was all sinew and laddered ribs. Laurel, angered by the interruption, used the makings on the bedstand to roll a cigarette, spilling tobacco over the sheet and her bare bosom showing above it.

Determinedly not looking at her, Stonewarden said: "Well, it ain't as if Frank and Jesse and them Youngers didn't invent it in Liberty last February. Leastwise, this here bunch didn't kill anybody, though Willard Ebert's dog Ulysses S. Grant will be limping from bitch to bitch for a spell."

"How many?" Miller tugged on his boots.

"Four or five. One at the door, one to watch the tellers and customers, one to empty the drawers, and one to bust open the safe with a pinch bar. Maybe one more to see to the horses. They rode out shooting. Reckon you missed the noise."

"I heard it. Thought it was some kids getting set for the Fourth. How much they get?"

"Elwin Olmstead says twelve thousand. I figure it's nearer nine. He's got him a young wife and she helped my Alice shake out the stores in St. Louis last year. Anyways, the one that did the talking shoved a five-spot greenback across the counter asking for change, then pulled a hogleg down on the head teller and told him to keep it coming."

The marshal grabbed his hat and jacket. "Well, you waiting for your whiskers to grow or what? Kick up Frank and see what kind of a posse you can scare up."

"Fifteen, counting Jubal Lansdale, who says he'll bury them we shoot at cost." Stonewarden's Indian black eyes gave up nothing. "I figured that's what you'd want me to do so I went and done it. Ain't nothing to the job I didn't do twicet before you ever came to town."

"Well, catching a bunch of daylight bank robbers will sure be one."

"What about me?" Laurel called out from the bed.

Miller placed some coins on the dresser on his way out.

Frank had the marshal's chestnut saddled in front of the office, where a large group of horsemen were gathering, their mounts protesting the heat and flicking their tails at the flies clouding around their rumps. Hatless as always, wearing the same shirt and trousers and suspenders he wore year round, the big deputy sat a drafthorse that with him astride it looked no larger than an ordinary mount. Miller jerked the Yellow Boy Henry rifle out of the saddle scabbard on the chestnut and inspected the magazine for rounds, then slid it back in and stepped into leather. Gathering the reins, he made his voice loud. "Who's got money in the bank?"

The group rumbled. A storekeeper whose gold-rimmed spectacles glittered under his hat brim spoke up. "None of us, now."

"Then you'll appreciate us taking as many of them as we can alive in case they buried it. Now, raise your right hands and say 'I do.' "

" 'I do' what?" a gray-moustached rancher wanted to know.

"What's it matter so long as it gets said?"

The horsemen said it. The storekeeper asked if they were going to get stars to wear.

"Hell, no. Unless you want to pay for the brass in taxes." When there was no response, Miller kicked the chestnut into the middle of the street and the group started north.

Stonewarden knew something of tracking, and after some milling around on the flats outside town he selected a set of prints with one cracked shoe as part of their quarry. But after ten miles the trail split, with the tracks going off in two directions. They drew rein. Stonewarden's black-whiskered face was a study in scowls.

"What do you think, split up?" Miller asked him.

"No, these town boys take all their grit from numbers. Less than ten to a posse and they'll flush like a covey of quail at the first shot. I say we stick with old Broken Shoe."

"Anybody get a good look at any of these boys?"

"Head teller said the one that did the talking looked Indian. But the only Indians he ever seen came off a tobacco can."

On the other side of noon the riders started picking their way across a sand flat, acres of longitudinal mounds of windswept sand whipped into brittle, frozen waves. For a change there was no wind, and the tracks stood out in a straight line as on a moonscape. They stopped to examine a crest with a piece broken out of it. Just beyond it a depression had been gouged out of the sand as if by a shovel. Tracks of a man's boots mingled with hoofprints before the trail started up again. Stonewarden stepped down to wander alongside it, looking down. Then he returned and mounted. "Pulled up lame. Somebody took himself a spill."

"Broken Shoe?" Miller asked.

"No, one of the others."

By sundown the bootprints started up again, leading the limping animal. At that point the trail divided a second time and the others peeled off to the west, leaving the injured horse and its master to continue alone.

"Clannish, these outlaws," Stonewarden observed dryly.

"No, it's the way," said Miller. "You don't throw away the whole spur just because one rowel is busted."

"I reckon you know the life better than me."

Miller ignored the comment. "What's ahead?"

"Kansas River. He'll be camping there directly. We get the rest we can swing by after and pick him up. He won't get much farther without a good horse."

"He could steal one."

"Ain't likely he'll find one up this way." Stonewarden dug out a plug of brown mule and tore off a chew. "Most of the money'll be with the rest if they didn't bury it."

"If they did, our friend up ahead will know where."

"Well, let's not split the posse."

"I like this fellow. Why don't I just stay on him and you take after the others with these town boys. It don't pan out I'll trail you in the morning."

"You want to come on him alone?"

"I ain't no town boy."

Stonewarden agreed with this reasoning and led the posse west into the red sun. Miller continued north. Three hundred yards farther on he spotted a dark mound that didn't strike him as part of the landscape and reined in to peer at it through the dying light. It was the carcass of a dun horse.

He started forward again at a walk. Smoke puffed above the carcass, followed an instant later by a sharp report, flattened a little in the level vastness of eastern Kansas. The bullet kicked up a geyser of sand a hundred feet short of the chestnut. Two more puffs, two more reports so close together they crackled. The second shot fell shorter than the first and the third dug in even with it. He patted the neck of the skittish chestnut and urged it on for another fifty feet, where it set its hoofs and refused to continue.

Miller didn't try to force the animal. He turned the reins twice around the saddlehorn and rested one leg across the pommel while he unleathered the Yellow Boy. He snugged the butt into his right shoulder, rested his cheek on the stock, and squeezed off a round. Just before the smoke obscured his view he saw the distant carcass jerk. The man behind it opened up twice more. Ignoring the shots, Miller sent two more into the center of the smoke.

"Stop shooting! I'm coming out!"

The shout carried no echo in the featureless terrain. Miller let it die completely before he lowered the Henry an inch.

"Let's see you, all of you. Stand up."

He hadn't bothered to shout, trusting it to carry. The light slipped a little before the man responded. A narrow figure rose from behind the dead horse, his shadow thirty yards long, an attenuated appendage with a pistol held high in one black hand.

"Get rid of the hardware and come walking."

The sun slipped lower. A piece of the figure flew off then and landed in the sand on the other side of the carcass. Its owner came around the far end and approached, moving very slowly.

"Come on, come on." Miller fired over his head, wanting him closer before he lost the light. After that the man moved faster. When they were twenty feet apart Miller told him to stop.

The marshal narrowed his lids, squinting through gathering shadow. The man facing him wore a stained Confederate campaign hat with a broad tattered brim and a coat whose sleeves gave out inches before his hands started. His narrow face was Indian except for the eyes, mud-colored and full of humor. The brightness of his grin was spoiled by a black iron tooth in front.

"Marshal Miller," Isham Eagle said, "I always said you was too smart to go on raiding the border your whole life."

"Howdy, Ish." Miller kept the Henry raised.

"You don't look any too surprised to see your old pard."

"Your right foot turns in some since you took that ball in the leg at Independence. It shows in your tracks. When I put it with what the head teller said about the one with the words being Indian I didn't figure it could be anyone else."

"Goddamn dun mare tore a muscle or my tracks'd be all you had. I cut its throat finally for cover. You forget how hard it is to hide here in Jayhawker country till you're back in it."

"You should of stuck with that old Ap."

"Hell, I traded him right after Kansas City. You was there; or was it Jim Quill? There, you see, you got so good I can't tell the two of you apart." He sobered. "Old Jim, the Yanks stretched his neck for that first little thing we done for the Major in Topeka. They said he raped and kilt that girl, only it wasn't him, it was one of them Starks done it."

"Where's the money, Ish?"

"Shit, I had it, you think I'd of tried shooting it out with you? I'd of split it and we'd both of us went home happy just for old times' sake."

"You didn't know it was me when you tried shooting it out."

"Hell I didn't. Why you think I picked Emporia when there's other better banks 'twixt here and Missouri? You made the Springfield paper with that way you handled that stole horse thing last winter. I read it and I says, 'Well, Isham, you ought to go pay your old pard a visit.' Only by the time I got there it was business."

"Your pards busted you?"

Eagle looked sad. "John, it ain't like it was with the militia. Your horse pulls up lame you're like a wounded wolf and no good to the pack. I had four guns on me before I could ask for my cut. That Luke, he just looks at me with that hat of his cocked over the hole where his ear was and says, 'Ish, we just ain't got time to divide it up. I'll get your cut to you later.' Later, like when Christ comes back."

"Luke Stark? You're riding with the Starks?"

"Them and that Barney Dee that rode in the Major's regiment. Hey, you kind of left us twisting after the Major died."

"It was over."

"I reckon. Things just got worse after that. Some of the others blamed you, said you took our luck with you. You didn't, though. It was the Major."

"How's Emma Ashford?"

"She went and married again."

That surprised him. "Not you."

"Not me, you called that right. Sam Woodlawn, can you feature it? All that time he was snorting after her and nobody knowed it till the war came and he just walked right in there and made her honest, which is what she wanted right along. The old goat, she made him shave off his whiskers. He's got no chin. Head just grows right up out of his collar like a apple core."

"Turn out your pockets, all of them."

The humor took a moment going out of the half-breed's eyes. "I told you I was bust. You calling me a liar?"

"Yes." Miller smiled for the first time. "And that's as good a thing as you been called, so get your back down and pull out them pockets."

After a moment Eagle started to comply. Miller twitched the rifle. "Slow."

"You seen me throw out my gun."

"Your saddle piece. You carried at least two as long as I know you."

The inspection yielded a pocket knife, the Navy Colt Miller remembered or one just like it, a brass derringer, and, most reluctantly, a thick fold of paper currency with a twenty on the outside.

"How much?" The marshal took it.

"Thousand."

"Even split?"

"Even as we could make it running." Eagle's expression was stony.

"Owner of the bank put it at twelve thousand."

"We got five and some change. I can't think why you put the posse on *us*." He watched Miller pocket the money. "What's a marshal make now?"

"Can't do it, Ish. Everybody knows everybody else and if I started spending this here they'd all know."

"Nobody said you had to stick."

"I took to the place."

"Well, how you fixing to get me *and* the money back to town?"

It was getting dark fast now. The two men's faces were in shadow.

"Over my horse's rump if I got to," Miller said.

"You don't want to, though, and the town don't insist on it. It's the money they want. You can say I made a fight of it and you buried me out here."

"They won't believe it."

"They won't care. Dip one end of the greenbacks in my dun's blood and they'll be glad enough to have it back they'll say you kilt the whole James-Younger Gang." The grin left his voice. "John, they'll hang me in Kansas."

Miller, balancing the rifle along his right forearm, lowered it a little. He could no longer see the front sight. "You'll stay clear of Emporia?"

"I ain't making no promises."

"I tell them I killed you and you come back, they'll hang *me*."

"They won't remember me. I'm just a no-account breed. How you think I lived this long?"

The marshal let the Henry drop the rest of the way. "Don't come back, Ish."

"I do you'll be first to know."

They parted there in the dark, neither seeing the other leave. Miller camped on the Kansas and returned to town the next day to learn that the posse still had not reported back. When he presented the bloodstained money and his story to Elwin Olmstead at the the Farmer's Trust, Daniel J. Black and Howard Rippert were among those present, and the little bearded man pumped Miller's hand as if he were drawing gold. From there the marshal went to Madame Phillipe's, where the story had already got to Laurel DePaul, who asked him if this visit was going on the marker with the rest.

Isham Eagle returned unrecognized to Emporia in January 1867.

CHAPTER FOURTEEN

They place a woman at the heart
of the fight at Lundgren's store;
One side claims she was just a tart,
the other, a full-blowed whore.

The sheriff of Lyon County was a Finn named Kussinen who had helped the governor get out the vote during the fiery election of 1864, only to be overlooked in the confusion of sorting out a minority victory and settling appointments magnanimously promised in the depths of a desperation campaign. In consolation, when the old sheriff died the following year Kussinen was hastily installed, with an eye to the next political round. As a firm Reconstruction Republican he was equally prized and despised in a county that had split down the middle on the slavery question in 1860. The firmly Democratic Emporia *Bulletin* greeted 1867 with an eight-column summation of Sheriff Kussinen's works thus far in his tenure with all the solemn fire of a Presbyterian minister judging the Prince of Lies. Historically, the election of 1868 would prove to be the last of its length, for with the completion of the transcontinental telegraph the following year it would be possible for the events of Monday in Washington City to become dinner-table conversation in California on Friday.

The *Bulletin* editor's name was G. W. Tiplady. The only son of a slave-owning family in Maryland, he had come West in the forties when the family's Baltimore shipping interests went down in the Horse Latitudes during an off-season hurricane and his grandfather blew off the top of his own skull with a flintlock pistol once owned by Henry Morgan. Tiplady had lost a leg and his first wife to a skirmish with Sioux warriors on his way West, fished his first printing press out of the Missouri River after his ferry overturned, and failed twice to

capture the Kansas Democratic gubernatorial nomination. He was a
lean, coarse-complexioned forty-eight with a tuft of chin whiskers
already gone white and a platinum watch chain dangling a fob fashioned from the flint arrowhead that had cost him his leg. His frequent
visits to Madame Phillipe's had led to the inevitable jokes about his
name at the Jackrabbit Saloon and speculation on what uses he made
of his mahogany peg on these occasions; but Madame Phillipe was
discretion itself, and speculation it remained.

John Miller heard the peg creaking and thumping the hardpack
inside the livery on New Year's Day while he was rubbing down his
chestnut after a morning's ride. When he confirmed it was the editor,
he bade him good morning and put away the Remington he had
leveled across the top of the stall.

Tiplady, who for reasons of his own affected a bad eye to go with
the missing limb, cocked his cold blue right one at Miller, who was
busy scrubbing the horse's lathered back with a worn towel. "One
would think such duty beneath a marshal's station," he said, "particularly when you're paying a nigger to do it for you."

"Mr. Tiplady, do you oil your own press, or do you trust that to the
help?"

"I stand outflanked. Have you a moment?"

"I got nothing but moments. This law work is like sitting around
watching corn get yellow."

"Journalism is hardly different. Waiting for news to happen, I pass
the time selling advertising, which necessitates adding pages upon
which to put more news for which I must wait to have happen. Did
you see today's number?"

"Over breakfast. You and the sheriff don't get on."

"He is a corrupt political hack. You know him of course."

"Ain't had that pleasure." Miller bent to work the towel briskly up
and down the chestnut's legs.

"I can't say I'm surprised. He has an office in town but he is never
there. Instead he holds court at his ranch outside the city limits,
where he raises horses on his share of the profits from his cousin Otto
Lundgren's whiskey-smuggling operation to the savages."

Miller, gently stroking the delicate hocks, thought marvelous the
editor's success in keeping emotion from his voice whenever the conversation turned to Indians. All through the war, he had been told,

Tiplady had published editorials calling for the Union to make peace with the Confederacy and join with Lee's army to destroy the Plains tribes. Rumor held he forced his second wife to dress and wear her hair after the example of the wife he had lost to the Sioux, but Miller discounted this. He suspected Helen Tiplady was naturally dowdy.

"I don't know Lundgren too good," the marshal said, straightening. "I know his partner, Fick Wilson."

"Yes-s," said Tiplady, holding on to the *s*.

Miller felt the sting of appearing stupid. It was no secret that both he and Wilson were paying attention to Laurel DePaul at Madame Phillipe's, or that Wilson had proposed to her, mainly to get one over on his rival the marshal. Fortunately she had refused. It got around then that she favored Miller. In reality she had balked at the idea of living with Wilson on his homestead up on the Kansas. Before that there had been another episode, much more sinister, in which the *Bulletin* had taken a hand.

"Mr. Tiplady, you ain't here just to spout off about Sheriff Kussinen. You got a newspaper for that."

"Quite right." The editor was looking at him with both eyes now. "As you know, I am the leader of the Democratic Party in this county."

"You *are* the Democratic Party in this county."

Tiplady mistook this for a statement of his influence. "I prefer to think of myself as its conscience," he said modestly. "We are now in the process of selecting a candidate to oppose the sheriff in the next election."

"That ain't till a year from November. Shouldn't you wait at least till the sparks go out from last night's fireworks?"

"News travels slowly out here. We must announce before March and file shortly thereafter. There is much work to be done. I can't do it all. A fair percentage of the constituency can't read. They use the *Bulletin* in their outhouses."

"Well, paper is scarce."

"Personal contact is crucial. The candidate must move around the county, introduce himself, shake every hand likely to mark an *X* on a ballot come the day. Rest assured, you will not be idle these next twenty-two months."

Transfixed by the editor's plodding journalistic style of speech, Miller caught the personal pronoun late. He noted first the ice blue eyes studying him intently; then heard the echo.

"Hold on. *Me?*"

"Why not? You are a lawman, which already qualifies you more than that boondoggle Kussinen. Moreover you are a hero. Certainly you read that much in my account of your darling duel with the leader of those bandits who ravaged the Farmer's Trust last summer. Come, do not ask me to accept that you gave no thought to political gain in such a climate."

The marshal scrutinized Tiplady's face, so like a goat's with its spray of chin plumage, glittering now with icicles from his vaporized breath in the cold of the stables. There had been no flicker of irony in his use of "daring duel" and "ravaged." He wondered how much the editor believed of what he was saying, or if he had been taken under the spell of his own words. He would come to know many writers and journalists, and to wonder the same thing about every one of them.

"What's it pay?" he asked then.

The question surprised the newspaperman. "I can look it up for you. Better, certainly, than your present position. Then there are other added benefits, not, er, provided for in the charter." He cleared his throat, warming up. But Miller interrupted.

"They better be enough, Mr. Tiplady, because you see when you walked in on me I was thinking on turning the whole works here over to Jack Stonewarden and riding on. There is just too much time between goings-on in this work. I suspect sheriffing is the same."

"Certainly not. As marshal you are expected solely to keep the peace. As sheriff you would be chief administrator of the county, empowered to levy taxes, call special elections, settle property disputes—"

"Sheriff's in charge of taxes?"

"Subject, of course, to review by the governor in the event of an appeal," Tiplady clarified. "But that requires time. In the meanwhile the sheriff wields an influence over his fellow residents similar to that of a feudal baron over his tenants." He leaned forward. The peg creaked. "Well, Marshal? Have I succeeded in arousing your sense of public duty?"

"I'm trying to figure where you gain."

"The administrator's appointments will of course be in keeping with party policy." He framed the words as if by rote.

Miller went on rubbing down places he'd already rubbed until the chestnut complained. He crumpled the towel and tossed it onto the pile near the stable door to grow stiff with the others.

"I'll get back to you, Mr. Tiplady."

The editor adjusted his hat, soft black with a curled brim. "The headline announcing your decision to run is set and locked in the chase. You have but to give me the word and my subscribers will read of it that day. We stand, Marshal Miller, on the threshold of political history. Let's make an effort not to stumble." He left, thumping and creaking.

When Isham Eagle returned to Emporia, one week after G. W. Tiplady's conversation with John Miller, his first stop was at the Farmer's Trust, where he pretended interest in the portraits of Andrew Johnson and George Washington mounted on the wall opposite the counter until the head teller's cage was free. Then he stepped before it.

Changes had been made since his last visit. Where there had been open counter, across which a customer could shake the teller's hand or poke a pistol in his face and demand money, an oaken barrier rose six feet from the floor with varnished bars in the spaces where the employees met the public. The soft black iron safe had been replaced by a walk-in vault built into the back wall with a big square steel door, and a hard-eyed character with a Smith & Wesson in an open holster stood by the street door giving everyone the dangerous look. It all appeared very formidable, but there was still room to shove a barrel between the bars, and if it came to shooting, wood was no match for the .44 caliber ball fired by the Army Colt Eagle had been carrying since Miller had confiscated his .36 Navy and the big saddle gun he had carried for twelve years. By that time the guard would be either dead or under the gun, because no man could be ready all the time, and the men it was his business to be ready for would come in ready. But the Jameses and Youngers had been busy since Liberty, and an institution dependent on its customers' confidence had to show something.

The teller Eagle had selected, thirty and balding, with a toothbrush moustache and green-tinted rimless glasses, was the same man whose brains he had threatened to plaster over the back wall last June if he didn't stand clear while his companions emptied the drawers and safe. Now as then, the half-breed introduced himself by sliding a five-dollar note under the cage and asking for change. Looking right at him, the teller said: "Yes, sir. Will that be coins or notes?"

Eagle smiled, not showing his iron tooth. "Coins. I like money I can hear."

The exchange completed, they thanked each other and Eagle walked away. Part of it, he knew, was the way he looked. He had traded his Confederate hat and worn homespun for a new Stetson with a pinched crown and a black coat and gray vest with striped pants, the Colt's ivory handle secreted like a gentleman's beneath the coat. His hair was cut and his nails were trimmed. The rest of it was attitude: go in thinking clean thoughts and nine times out of ten that was how they took you.

He unhitched his horse from the rail in front of the bank, got directions to the livery, and led it there. It was a chesty bay gelding with fat haunches and a corn-fed belly, a cross-country runner, not much for speed in a sprint but a world-beater for endurance over the long run. He had won it in a trey-high bluff at a table in Junction City and had refused two hundred dollars for it from an easterner who had been watching the game. So far it had won him that much in races, not to mention his life when he fled Leavenworth after someone heard dice rattling in his pocket. The hell of it was he hadn't gotten the chance to palm the legitimate pair and replace them with his own before he was discovered. Since then he had taken to pocketing them separately.

The route to the livery led him past the marshal's office, where he nodded a greeting to a big, side-whiskered man coming out with a star on his coat. He had the look of a man accustomed to handing out orders, not accepting them. Eagle wondered with a sudden twinge if Miller had moved on. But he had no wish to call attention to himself at this stage by asking straight out, and so he led the bay on past. The side-whiskered man followed his progress with eyes Indian black.

The Negro at Carson's Livery rolled his eyes in an affected way when he saw the handsome horse and recommended the Good Samaritan as a hotel for gentlemen. Eagle flipped him one of the silver

dollars he had gotten from the bank, unlimbered his bedroll and
scuffed valise, and carried them to the place named. There a young
clerk with a stiff collar and pomade in his dark hair slid off a stool
behind the front desk and folded the newspaper he had been reading
to register the new arrival. Seeing Eagle's face, he drew back the pen
he had offered. "Are you an Indian?"

He had one of those accents that smelled of lobster and lawn
tennis. Eagle said, "No, I'm a Creole from New Orleans."

"Oh. Sorry."

Eagle took the pen, dipped it fresh, and signed the register with a
practiced flourish. "That John Miller's name I seen in that headline?"
He nodded at the newspaper.

"Yes. The marshal has announced his candidacy for county sheriff.
He is G. W. Tiplady's Great Democratic Hope this election." The
clerk was too well-bred to sneer, but it was in his words.

"Any chance he'll win?"

"Not if decency and the spirit of John Brown prevail." The clerk
made a show of looking right and left and leaned forward across the
desk. They were alone in the lobby. "Tiplady is a slaver."

"Hell you say. I thought that trash was run out of Kansas for good."

"Oh, they continue to plague us. Sixteen." He laid a key in front of
Eagle.

"Where can I buy a paper?"

"Take mine. It's just a secessionist rag anyway."

"Well, thank you."

"My job is to make our guests welcome, Mr."—he glanced at the
register—"Dubonneut."

The half-breed picked up the key and the newspaper, hoisted his
belongings, and went up to room sixteen to read the *Bulletin* and wait
for Miller to call.

It was a short wait. He had just finished reading and was using the
pen and ink provided by the hotel to correct the anatomy of the
women in the advertising engravings when the knock came. Stretched
out on top of the bed in his shirtsleeves and stockinged feet, he put
down the paper, took the big Army off the nightstand, and called for
the visitor to enter.

Miller came in wearing the big hat and buffalo coat Eagle had seen him in last and holding a long-barreled Remington. He looked at Eagle's gun and leaned the door shut behind him.

"Dubonnet?" he said.

"Doo-bun-*no*," Eagle corrected. "Leastwise, that's how the man I got it from pronouced it. He ain't using it no more. How the hell are you, John?" He let down the hammer and put the gun back on the nightstand.

Miller held on to his. "Mad as bedamned, same as I was last summer. What are you doing back?"

"I had to clear my mind. Knowing there's a place you can't go back to, it's like having a blind spot, or looking out on open prairie and seeing a fence around one part of it. It grinds your gut."

"What are you doing back really?"

Eagle's iron tooth caught the light. He slapped the newspaper. "I see where you're in politics now. That at all like war?"

"I won't know for a while. I just announced. One thing's sure, I can't afford having the voters see a bandit I killed in June walking around town in January."

"You fixing to do it a second time?"

Miller stroked the Remington's hammer with the ball of his thumb. "No." He let it down and holstered the weapon. "I'd have just as hard a time explaining how the body got up here and looking so fresh. So I'll just ask you to cut your business short and find a good road out of town."

"John, I didn't figure you to be one to get religion."

"It ain't religion. It's politics, like I said."

"What if I told you I just made change at the bank I robbed last time and the same teller didn't know me from Robert E. Lee?"

"I'd say it was the clothes. When he's thought on it some he'll put you to the robbery. That's why I want you gone, before he ties it up."

"No, if he remembers at all now he'll fix it to a customer he changed a note for. Say, I hear that posse of yours made a short piece of that Barney Dee that helped us with the bank."

"They just scraped up what the Starks left. You're lucky your horse pulled lame. Their mother never taught them the virtue of sharing."

"Once we made the cut they never seen my back. That bunch was square during the fighting, but peace is hard on some folks' characters." Eagle brightened. "Anyway, I reckon that's good for your chances of office, you being the only one to bring back any part of the money. I'm thinking you could be more grateful, seeing as how it was my cut."

"I could of blowed a hole in you big enough to drive a wagon and team through and took it anyway. The longer I look at you the more I think that's what I should of done."

"Well, since I'm here we can talk about what use you can make of that."

Something in Eagle's tone poked at Miller's curiosity. He said, "After Jack Stonewarden told me about this gussied-up breed he seen leading a good horse I went over to Carson's and the nigger said where you was staying. I seen the horse. You've come up some in just a few months."

"I give up life on the scout, if that's what's worrying you," Eagle said. "It's hell on the nerves and the food's no good. I got me a trade now." He reached inside his vest. Miller came up with the Remington. Slowly, Eagle drew out a deck of cards and held it up.

"Tinhorning?" The marshal put away the gun a second time. "I had you down for something less chancy, like blowing the safe in the telegraph office."

"Oh, I shade the odds a mite." He shuffled the cards idly, expertly.

"You can do that anywhere."

"I spent half my life moving around. I'm looking for a permanent spot, a steady table someplace where I don't bother the law and the law don't bother me. I looked over that Jackrabbit Saloon coming in. If I can cut a deal with the management I can sell my saddle and get old."

"The Jackrabbit is Stonewarden's property. Part of it is."

"I can split three ways. You don't need as much when you stick."

Miller leaned back against the door and crossed his boots. "What's one third come to?"

"Well, it varies. Hundred a month when it's good. 'Course, now, that's just one game."

"Spit it out, Ish. How many games we talking about?"

"How many are there in town?"

The marshal paused, actually counting. A slow grin lifted his tawny moustaches. "Sheriff Kussinen will howl. His cousin Otto Lundgren and Lundgren's partner, Fick Wilson, run half of Emporia out of the general store on the north end. He'll take it as a challenge."

"Well, what's this?" Eagle slapped the paper again.

"That's politics."

"Guns and money," said Eagle. "Out here that's politics."

CHAPTER FIFTEEN

Seven men met before that place,
just three walked away;
Seven hands entered the deadly race,
four pairs were folded away.

Fick Wilson was three years Miller's junior. Abandoned as an infant by his unmarried mother, he had been rescued half frozen from an ash can by a policeman behind the New York City offices of Fick & Wilson Importers, which names the nuns gave him at the orphanage where he was taken after the hospital was through with him. He ran away from there at fifteen and joined the Army of the Potomac, lying about his age, fought with competence but little distinction during the early campaigns of the war, was captured at the second battle of Bull Run and sent to the Andersonville hellhole. There a brutal beating by a sadistic guard gave him the gap-toothed grin so familiar to those who knew him later and the foul diet ruined his stomach forever for all but the blandest foods. Other trials, never related by him, had turned his hair white and left him a facial twitch that some, John Miller included, read as a sign that his reason was gone. In truth, he had a violent temper and had killed two men in separate incidents that his friend Sheriff Kussinen had ruled acts of self-defense. Future generations would come to associate his name with a bone-thin corpse photographed in a satin-lined casket with his pale hair oiled down and his dark moustache waxed into curls and more wax plugging a hole in his forehead.

His association with Otto Lundgren, Kussinen's cousin, began shortly after he arrived in Emporia, among the first wave of veterans cut loose to drift after Lee's surrender. Lundgren was just then beginning to trade in whiskey and the odd shipment of rifles with the Sioux and northern Cheyenne for the beadwork and buffalo robes becoming popular in the East, and he needed a man with the sand to face both the hostiles and the U.S. Cavalry, whose job it was to stop the illegal trading. Since any fear that Wilson might have known had been beaten out of him in Andersonville, he accepted the challenge, and after three successful trips had demanded and was granted a full partnership in the operation. By this time he had been questioned by soldiers in connection with a skirmish between a cavalry patrol and a band of suspected whiskey traders in which three troopers were slain, but had been released when the sheriff announced that he and Wilson had dined together that evening at Kussinen's horse ranch outside Emporia. Sheriff Kussinen played chess with the commander of Fort Leavenworth the first Tuesday of every month.

Fick Wilson was as good a man with a revolver as John Miller had ever seen.

The first recorded confrontation between the whiskey runner and the marshal took place in June 1866, when Miller called on Wilson in the latter's town residence at the Emporia House and removed Laurel DePaul from the room at gunpoint. Wilson, in a naked condition at the time, offered no resistance, and the woman returned obligingly to Madame Phillipe's, where custom smiled on both rivals visiting her at different times. The second, in September of that year, was more serious. Spotting Wilson on a deserted street one night after curfew, Miller snapped off a shot that went wide in the poor light and shattered a sign over the apothecary. Wilson, unarmed, ran away into the shadows. Although Miller claimed he had fired at a rat, a witness who had observed the incident through his hotel-room window disputed him. The sheriff sent deputies to arrest the marshal, who met them at the office door with a shotgun. They returned empty-handed. By then the *Bulletin* had come out in support of Miller's action against a known whiskey trader caught outside after curfew, and the sheriff, mindful of his electors, chose not to pursue the matter.

The incident of Wilson's proposal of marriage to Laurel and of her refusal had become local folklore and appeared to cancel itself out. But shortly after announcing his intention to run for sheriff, Miller bent to pick up his pool cue during a game on the ground floor of the Good Samaritan Hotel just as a bullet disintegrated the plate-glass street window, missing him by inches and plowing a furrow in the felt on the table. The culprit had fled by the time anyone reached the street. There were no witnesses, and this time Otto Lundgren stepped in to say that Fick Wilson was playing poker with him in the store at the time of the shooting. This story was backed up by two other players, both employees of Lundgren's.

"I'm just glad he's no better of a shot than I am," Miller commented, during a meeting in the parlor of Jack Stonewarden's house on the edge of town that evening. Mrs. Stonewarden had retired upstairs a few minutes earlier.

G. W. Tiplady, who had suggested the meeting, was the only one not seated. He paced the room in a kind of sailor's roll, his peg thudding out of rhythm with his one foot as he followed the pattern in the oval rug. Stonewarden sat in his big easy chair blowing rings from his after-dinner cigar and Miller half lay on the settee with one leg hooked over the arm. Isham Eagle, there at the marshal's invitation under his Michel Dubonneut pseudonym, occupied a straight-backed parlor chair in the corner, counting the figures on the wallpaper next to him in preparation for a bet. His black coat and striped pants had begun to conform to his angular construction.

"Pistols are for close shooting," said Tiplady, who carried a derringer in his vest pocket. "In any case, it's obvious to me, even if it isn't to you, that Wilson has agreed to remove you as a threat to Kussinen next year. I regard this as a happy assessment of our chances."

Miller said, "Laurel thinks it's her he's after. She's been capering like a girl in a novel ever since this thing got started."

"Let's don't talk about her till Rose is asleep," Stonewarden cautioned.

Tiplady ignored him. "A quaint notion, and doubtless that's how the damnable dime novelists would see it. But Lundgren and Wilson stand to lose everything if you're elected sheriff. Without Kussinen's protection, the next time Wilson and the Army tangle, their business will collapse and they'll land in prison."

"You believe that, about prison?" asked Miller.

"Not really. There is too much money involved. But they will fear the worst. From now on, Marshal, I would advise great care for your safety."

"I walk in the shade and sit with my back to walls now. I get any more careful old Frank will be feeding me through the bars back of the office."

"Where *is* Frank?" Tiplady asked. "He should be here."

Stonewarden said, "No, he shouldn't. He'd just get confused. Hell, *I'm* confused. This law business used to be real simple before Miller got bit by the public-office bug."

"On the other hand, I haven't a notion why *he's* here." The editor pointed his chin-whiskers at Eagle.

"Mr. Dubonnet is an old friend and handy when there's trouble," said Miller. "I'd deputize him, only he won't have any."

The man under discussion tilted his head. "I got a gold double eagle says there's more than a hunnert half-moons on that wall. Any takers?"

"He's unpalatable to the voters. I haven't the journalistic skill to dress up a gambler and a half-breed Indian." For once Tiplady was unable to suppress the rage in his tone.

"I'm a Basque."

"Basques are Spanish. Your name is French."

Eagle looked sad. "I don't ask you about *your* maw."

"Dubonnet stays," Miller said.

Tiplady returned to the subject. "I could hire you a bodyguard."

"Bodyguards always get in the last word in an argument, never the first. Besides, who'd you get that's better than me or Fick Wilson?" The marshal looked at his deputy. "Who's with us if we make a fight of it?"

"That would be political suicide," Tiplady said. "Kansas has had enough of killing after ten years."

It was Stonewarden's turn to ignore the editor. "Rippert and Black, maybe, though they're both of them Republicans so I can't say for sure. Jube Lansdale, he's game for anything that makes funerals, being an undertaker. Us here and Frank. That's eight."

"Don't count *me.*"

"Don't stamp that damn stick leg while Rose is asleep," Stonewarden barked.

"If I can I want to keep the civilians clear of it," said Miller. "Make it look more lawlike."

"Even if you won, the victory would be hollow, because the electorate would come out against you in force next year."

The marshal regarded Tiplady. "This here is our work, my deputy's and Dubonnet's and mine. Lundgren and Wilson don't care shit about us in the election. It's business. I'd count it a favor if you'd stick to politics and leave the gun talk to us."

"You don't consider your friend the Basque a civilian?" Stonewarden put out his cigar in the candy dish he used for an ashtray.

"Mike Dubonnet's Mike Dubonnet. He swings either way."

Tiplady pulled on his hat. "I'm leaving."

"We want to catch them in town then," the deputy said. "Lundgren's got too many friends outside. We're talking about Lundgren too, ain't we? Him and Wilson?"

The front door slammed. Miller nodded thoughtfully. "Them and whoever else is with them at the time, on anything not legitimate business. You do a thing you got to do it proper and with no ends flapping loose. Ain't that what you taught me, Mike?"

Eagle, playing blackjack with himself on a pedestal table he had pulled close, said right. Miller nodded again, distracted. He had almost called him Ish.

Whatever he was called, neither Eagle nor any of the others took any action for the rest of the week. Fick Wilson was out of town, ostensibly on a freighting trip for Lundgren, probably staying invisible in the wake of his unsuccessful attempt on the marshal's life. "Where is 'Dry Gulch' Wilson?" demanded the *Bulletin*, at the head of a four-column account of the cowardly attempt, complete with boldly subheaded passages reminding readers of the would-be assassin's ties to Otto Lundgren and the sheriff. Meanwhile Eagle dealt shaved cards at the Jackrabbit and hulking Frank swept out the cells behind the marshal's office and Miller and Stonewarden broke up a gang of schoolboys assaulting pedestrians on Main Steet with snowballs.

Miller spent most of Friday night arguing with Laurel DePaul, who wanted to know why he didn't take her off the line and set her up in a house for just the two of them. He left her room at three, slept in the cramped quarters off the cells that the city provided, and dragged into the office at six, bleary-eyed and with his head hammering. He boiled yesterday's coffee on the barrel stove and was behind the desk sipping his second cup of the thick black stuff when Stonewarden entered, brushing snow off his shoulders and hat.

"Wilson's back," he said.

Miller fished a bottle half full of whiskey out of a drawer cluttered with empties and poured a slug into the cup. Corking the bottle: "When'd he get in?"

"Last night, I reckon. He's over at the store. I seen him through the window."

"Anybody with him?"

"Just Lundgren's all I seen. There may be more."

"All right. Roll out Frank while I fetch Ea—Dubonnet." He drained the cup, made a face when the contents hit bottom, and got up to reach for his hat and buffalo coat.

"Watch your step. We got eight inches last night."

The fresh fluffy snow was pink in the light of dawn. Miller waded through the calf-high stuff to the other side of the street, turned the corner, and went through the lobby of the Good Samaritan without speaking to the clerk. He pounded on the door of room sixteen until a woman gasped inside, then told Eagle to climb off whoever it was and get dressed, explaining why. Three minutes later the half-breed came out, buttoning his vest. They returned to the office—Eagle cursing the wet snow soaking through his new hand-tooled boots—and found Jack Stonewarden and Frank dressed for outside. The big half-wit wore a bearcoat that made him look twice as huge and a farmer's plug hat a size too small that rode on top of his shaggy head like a peach tin on a high wave.

Miller unlocked the gun case and handed out shotguns all around. "Thought you was stuck on pistols," said Stonewarden. He loaded his shotgun from the drawer under the cabinet.

"Pistols are for carrying around when you don't know when trouble's going to come or where. Scatterguns are too heavy for that, but they come handy when you do know."

Eagle laid his on the desk while he inspected the cylinder of his Army Colt. "I may just run with Katy here when it gets hot. Last time I shot a twelve-gauge when I wasn't ready, it dislocated my shoulder."

"Use your hip," said Miller. "We're shooting men, not ducks."

Stonewarden said, "What's our reason for going to Lundgren's?"

"He's still got his sign hanging low, ain't he?"

"Last I looked."

"Well, there's an ordinance against that. I told him to raise it."

"Sounds a poor excuse to kill a man."

"Two old men shaking their beards at each other is a poorer one. But a million men spent four years killing each other over it." Miller slammed shut his shotgun's breech. "Let's go."

The sun was pale now behind thickening clouds. Snow fell lightly, tiny flakes swirling like cigar ash in a cold wind but stinging like bits of glass when they touched the faces of the four men walking along the boardwalk with shotguns. Although the streets were empty at that hour, lights had come on in some of the upper windows. The segmented front window of Lundgren's store at the north end of the block was the only one lit at street level. As the four approached, a powerful gust came around the corner and rattled the panes like thunder.

"Door's opening," said Eagle.

"Hit the street. Spread out."

But the other three were moving before Miller gave the orders. By the time Otto Lundgren came out in a wolfskin hat and coat, the four were standing in snow over their boot tops with four feet separating them, shotguns clasped to their hips. The storekeeper took a step, stopped, started to back up, then planted his feet with the open door spilling out light behind him.

"What you doing, Marshal, hunting?"

Lundgren was a heavy man in his fifties with great white moustaches that drooped together like folded wings to cover his mouth and chin. He had pale lashes and blue eyes that were almost silver against a high year-around flush. His hands were hidden in the big pockets of his coat. Miller told him to take them out slowly.

He didn't move. "Why, what is the problem?"

"Just do what I said."

"Are you arresting me? For what?"

"I don't see Wilson," Stonewarden muttered.

The marshal raised his voice. "Where's your partner?"

"Fick? He is out freighting."

"I say he ain't. Now, get them hands out where I can see them."

"I think I have a right to know why you are doing this."

"I told you before to raise that sign as a hazard. Now we're here to enforce the ordinance."

Lundgren turned to look at the sign hanging over the boardwalk, taking his hands out of his pockets as he moved. At that instant glass crashed above him and Stonewarden cried out and fell. Eagle shouted, threw away his shotgun, and swung up his revolver, flame licking out the muzzle. Miller's shotgun roared at the same time. Fick Wilson dropped his gun through the shattered second-story window, his chest gone and his forehead pierced dead center. His missing front teeth turned his grimace into a cartoon. Meanwhile Frank opened up on Lundgren, who was lifted off his feet by the blast and hurled back through the open door.

"Side door!" yelled Eagle.

A slight figure in shirtsleeves and garters emerged into the alley between the store and the post office next to it with his hands raised, facing the gun men. Miller recognized him as Lundgren's bookkeeper even as he was blowing the man almost in half with his other barrel. The clerk landed on his back in the snow, where he lay flopping like a fish.

Wind whistled through the sudden silence.

The fight had lasted less than thirty seconds. In its aftermath, big Frank sank to his knees in the deep snow, hugging Jack Stonewarden's bullet-broken head to his chest and making little mewing noises that were chilling coming from a man his size. Miller looked from him to the much smaller man convulsing in the alley, lifted his eyes to regard Wilson's arm hooked over the bullet-chewed windowsill, and inclined his head toward Otto Lundgren's bulk lying across the threshold. Eagle bounded up onto the boardwalk and stood over the storekeeper for a few seconds with his gun out. Then he lowered it.

"His hands are empty," he said. "He didn't have nothing in them pockets but his hands."

"Then he should of took them out the first time I told him." Miller plucked the smoking shells from his shotgun's breech and locked it.

Across the street, in the office of the Emporia *Bulletin*, G. W. Tiplady turned from the front window to greet his assistant, who had just thundered down from his quarters over the office with his shirttail out and his high-topped shoes in one hand. The editor had finished running up the blind just as the shooting started.

"Set a head," he snapped, seating himself behind his writing desk. "Fourteen points. 'Retribution in the Streets.' I'll have the first column written by the time you've locked it in."

CHAPTER SIXTEEN

In flight again, he packed his gear
and laid his star to rest;
And on his door for those come near
he hung a sign: "Gone West."

Jubal Lansdale left the corpses in the window of his funeral parlor for three days. He used paint and pomade and stopped up with wax the holes that showed and dressed them in their Sunday best and took money from the town photographer in return for the privilege of making a picture, prints of which went for a dollar apiece, black-bordered frame included. Supporters of Sheriff Kussinen bought one and reproduced it in a broadside with a bold heading fashioned after the *Bulletin*'s RETRIBUTION IN THE STREETS, but with the word "Murder" substituted for "Retribution." Asked by the newspaper to respond to the canard, John Miller commented merely that there had been only one street involved.

The bookkeeper, whose name was Thomas Keogh, was not part of the display. He lived for several hours with his belly full of lead pellets and laudanum and his body was claimed the next day by his sister, who drove in from Council Grove with her husband. When G. W. Tiplady tried to get a comment from her, the husband knocked him off his peg. They returned home that day with the coffin in the wagon box.

Fick Wilson and Otto Lundgren were buried in a double ceremony that involved a procession through the streets of Emporia, made up of most of the county's Republican leaders and Wilson's freighters, the latter in black armbands with the butts of their pistols showing. In contrast to all this gaudy solemnity, Rose Stonewarden had her husband interred in a simple graveside service attended by the marshal,

Tiplady, loyal Democrats, and Frank, wearing a tight black coat over
his work shirt and suspenders and blubbering like an overgrown calf.
The widow stood silent and motionless throughout the ceremony in a
black dress and thick veil. When Miller approached her afterward to
offer comfort, she turned away and went to her waiting carriage,
where a friend of Stonewarden's who had taken no part in the political fight started the horse moving.

Two days after the service, Sheriff Kussinen paid a call on the
marshal in his office.

Miller recognized him immediately, although the two had never
met. Kussinen's bushy brows and burnsides, combed straight out from
his cheeks like gray awnings, were visible in stacks of election posters
awaiting pickup at the post office, and his rotund figure had been
prominent in the carriage directly behind the hearse carrying the
bodies of Lundgren and Wilson to the cemetery. Aside from his
breadth he bore little resemblance to his cousin the storekeeper, his
eyes dark under the remarkable thatch of brow and crowded into the
shadows of a great prow of nose that ended in a bulb. He had the lips
of a voluptuary and chins enough for three. He was just Miller's
height.

"I've been remiss in not introducing myself earlier," he observed,
lowering his soft fat into the chair on the public side of the desk with
the aid of a gold-knobbed stick. "I plead the trials of office on top of
the demands of maintaining a successful ranching operation."

Miller said nothing. Kussinen had on a gray broadcloth overcoat
with velvet-faced lapels over a black suit of fine wool. A gold watch
chain strung with organizational affiliations described a glittering letter *J* from a vest pocket to the seam where buttons struggled to
contain his flesh. A diamond threw off colored lights from the plump
little finger of his left hand.

"A sad business, this thing at the store," he went on. "And entirely
unnecessary. I wish you'd come to me before you got in with this
Tiplady person. I would have made better use of you."

"As what, your va-let?"

The great brows wriggled, gray caterpillars over close dark eyes.
"You haven't the temperament for politics, Marshal. The voters don't
appreciate irony."

"What happened at Lundgren's didn't have nothing to do with

politics. Him and Wilson took exception to me and Mike Dubonnet nailing down most of the gambling in town. You too, I expect."

"You know that and I know that. Our respective party stalwarts, however, view it as practice for what promises to be an interesting November 1868. At the grass roots the romantic notion persists that you and the late Mr. Wilson came to grips over the hand of a fair lady."

"Well, Laurel's price always was fair, but it wasn't her hand she was selling. Anyway, she was just our way of keeping score."

"The concept is beyond the grasp of the normal voter. In any case, the soiled dove's presence in the business has persuaded the Women's Betterment Society to join with vociferous Republicans in calling for your resignation. I need hardly explain to you that the Society's leaders are all married to members of the Emporia Businessmen's Alliance."

"If you didn't, I would of guessed."

"Thus, in the short space of a week, your support among the pillars of this community has eroded to the point where not only are your county aspirations in serious jeopardy, but your present position as well."

Miller had been toying with a straight pen from the brass buffalo standard on the desk. Now he socked it into its holder. "Say it, Sheriff."

"Resign with dignity and depart the county. In return I will see that you are compensated from the treasury for the loss of this month's wages and for the inconvenience of pulling up roots. Say, two hundred dollars. I have the notes with me." He patted his breast pocket.

"I say no, then what?"

Kussinen showed a pair of pink, meaty palms. "I am only a servant of the public. I have no control over the actions of outraged citizens."

"Well, why not leave the work to them and save two hundred dollars?"

"Emporia is but one small part of the electorate in Lyon County. A lynching at the seat on top of four murders—excuse me, four killings —could split the ticket and land God knows who in office next year. This way we both benefit."

The marshal thumbed the brass star on his shirt absently. "Let me talk to Dubonnet. He's my partner. I'll get back to you."

"I thought you knew. Isham Eagle has left Emporia."

The words were a double shock, causing Miller's lips to part. The sheriff responded to the first.

"Marshal Miller, I've been in public life since the Van Buren administration. The Pinkertons have an extensive file on Mr. Eagle. As to his leaving, he checked out of the Good Samaritan this morning, before I came to call on him. The clerk gave me a message to give to you. Eagle told him you'd know what it meant." He fished a fold of hotel stationery out of the side pocket of his overcoat and hooked on a pair of gold-rimmed spectacles. " 'I'm going back to the place I keep to go back to. See you.' " He peered over the rims. "Can you make anything of that?"

"Yeah. It means someone ain't as married as you might think. You said three hundred?"

Kussinen started to correct him, then spread his thick lips in a broad politician's grin. "Yes. Three hundred was the amount."

"Maybe it was four."

"No, it wasn't that much."

"I had to ask," Miller said, unpinning the star from his shirt.

"Of course you did."

The farmer, big in old denims and a checked shirt softened by scrubbing and faded unevenly in strips where his suspenders rode, squinted through weather-cracks in his brown face at the visitor on the porch. When he did that he resembled their father. Very slowly the sun rose in his features.

"Eugene?"

Miller smiled wearily. "Howdy, Jerome."

"Dogs, it *is* you! Only it ain't Jerome, it's Matt." For an awkward moment he hesitated, twitching spasmodically in the lamplight coming from behind him. Then he threw a trunklike arm around Miller's shoulders and hauled him inside. "Ellen! Ellen, come and meet my brother Gene."

"Gene?" A stout young blond woman with high color in her cheeks and the beginnings of a second chin turned from the stove, wiping her hands on her apron. A smile flickered.

"Ellen's after your time," Matt said. "Her folks bought the old LoBrutto place. We got married last year."

"Year before," she corrected. "Pleased to meet you, Gene. Matthew he talks about you all the time."

Miller fidgeted, feeling watched. They were looking at a smallish man in snow-stiffened clothes with a moustache that wanted trimming and a mat of neglected whiskers on his cheeks, ravages of the long ride. He remembered his hat and took it off. Some sunburned skin came off with it.

"I can't feature you're Matt," he said. "You got so big." He had had enough education in politics not to say "old." The younger of his two brothers was, let's see, twenty-one or -two. He looked forty.

"You ought to see Jerome. What do you think of the way we fixed up the old place?"

He hadn't noticed anything different. The loft was where it had always been, with the ladder leading up to it, and the table was still standing where his mother toted up the bills and where his father had died after his fight with the mule. The circular rug was new, green and yellow in concentric circles. He remembered bare floor. "Looks smaller."

"That's just because you're bigger. Not much, though. Haw-haw. That window's new. Ellen wanted more light. And we built on a room in back for Ma."

"Is Ma here?"

"She's always here." Matt paused. "She had a stroke last year, Gene. She can't move or talk."

They went through a door that had been cut under the loft, leaving Ellen in the main room. The added-on part was much smaller, just big enough to contain a bed and a hard chair and a chest of drawers that Miller recognized from his parents' bedroom. Curtains were drawn over the single window, plunging the room in almost total darkness with the dusk. The air had a sweetish smell that Miller equated with old people.

Matt struck a match and lit the lamp standing on the chest. Light slid over the figure under the covers. A mop of hair gone nearly all gray, a bony face, a prominent chin. The woman lay as unmoving as a corpse except for her eyes, which were open and animated. They moved from Miller's brother to Miller. He saw that they saw him.

"You can talk to her," Matt said quietly. "Doc says she understands."

Miller said nothing. After two long minutes he stirred. His brother took the hint and blew out the lamp. They went back into the big room.

"She looks old, Matt. She can't be fifty."

"She's just fifty. It was losing Maureen done it. You know Maureen died." He looked anxious.

"I heard. I'm sorry I wasn't here."

"You couldn't of done nothing. Well, she just stopped caring after that. Old Henry busted his back keeping the place going—he died out there in the field—but it didn't mean nothing to her no more. That's when Jerome and I took over. Jerome, he turned out a disappointment. He went and joined up with the Army in '62 and didn't come back."

"Killed?"

"No, we got a letter from him when he mustered out. One page, and him gone three years. Said he was going to Texas to raise cows. It didn't sound like him at all. I was counting on him coming back. This place is too much for one man and I can't afford to hire no one." The anxious look returned. "You back now, Gene? I can sure use you."

"No, I'm headed west myself after this. I just swung back this way to visit."

"What's out there? Just desert."

"Maybe, maybe not. I ain't seen enough of it to tell. But desert or not, there's work for me."

"As who, John Miller?"

The brothers looked at each other. Matt's eyes were quick in their slits, like their mother's. "We been reading about you," he said. "The war and that thing in Kansas. I didn't feature you for any of it, Gene. I mean, that thing with that boy Curly, it was bad, but I could put reason to it. Them others . . ." He trailed off.

"You got to be in it to see it. It's like farming. It ain't for everybody."

After a moment, Matt brightened. "Say, you got to see little Bill. I bet you didn't know you was an uncle."

"He's asleep," Ellen said, poking a fork into a roast neck of venison. She slid it back into the oven and swung shut the door.

"Well, wake him up. This here's family."

She went through the curtains that had masked Miller's parents' bed and came out a minute later with a baby wrapped in a yellow blanket. It was red, with wisps of hair like cornsilk, and looked like every other baby Miller had ever seen. He said, "Hey, he's a beauty."

"You can hold him if you want," she said.

"No, thanks."

"Aw, go ahead," prodded Matt. "He's a Morner. He won't break."

"I said no."

It came out sharper than intended. A hole opened in the baby's face and it began bawling. Miller muttered an apology, but Ellen said: "No, he's hungry."

She sat down at the table cradling the child and unbuttoned her blouse. It was where Miller's mother used to sit when she nursed Maureen. He turned away.

Matt said, "Can't you do that in the bedroom? You're embarrassing Gene."

He put his chestnut in the barn and fed it and ate with them, his first hot meal in days, and slept in his old bed in the loft among odds and ends of farmhouse accumulation stored there since the last time the room had been used. The next day he helped his brother stack bales of straw in the barn to protect the horses from the cold. He noted that Matt owned no mules.

"Planted wheat last autumn," his brother told him, taking him on a walking tour of the farm, yellow showing in patches where the snow had receded. "They got this new kind now that grows in winter. That's the big crop here now. Pa wouldn't like it. He thought it a sin not to plant your land in everything you can."

Miller pointed. "You see that rockpile? There's two hundred and sixteen rocks in that pile. I counted every one."

"There's more now. Damn things grow up out of the ground like weeds. That'll be Bill's job when he's big enough."

"It's good work for a boy."

Miller's mother lived on soup and fresh milk, acquired from the farm next door in return for eggs from the chickens Ellen kept behind the house in a shelter Matt had built. Ellen held up her head with one hand and spoon-fed her, a spoonful of hot soup followed by a spoonful of cold milk. She explained that she had stopped using a glass for the milk after the paralyzed woman almost choked last summer. Miller stood at the foot of the bed and said nothing.

The baby started crying in the other room, a harsh, rasping bellow.

"He needs changing." Ellen looked up at Miller. "Finish for me?"

He hesitated, but she was already out of the chair and setting the bowl on the tray containing the glass of milk on the chest. He held his position for a moment after the door closed. His mother's eyes were on him. He came around the end of the bed then and sat down and picked up the bowl and spoon. When he lifted her head, her hair felt brittle against his palm. He put the spoon to her lips and waited, but they didn't move, couldn't move. He tipped it. The contents spilled over her chin and onto her nightdress. He found a napkin, used it on her chin, and inserted the next spoonful carefully between her lips. The liquid strained through her teeth. The muscles in her throat worked. He tried another, then the milk. He kept going until both vessels were empty.

He got up and lifted the tray. Then he set it back down. For a moment he looked at his mother, whose gaze met his. He sat down again and said, "I don't know how much they told you about me. Not much, I reckon; I reckon you know some of it anyway. You always did."

Her face was nearly as white as the pillow behind her head. Only her eyes seemed alive.

"I've killed me some men," he said. "Not any that didn't deserve killing, but that won't mean nothing to you. I've told my share of lies and been with easy women. I can't be what you set out in that letter you wrote. I tried it but it was like the stirrups was adjusted for somebody else's legs. You said once men without souls are needed out there. I reckon I'm one of them and that's why I can't stay."

He wanted to say more. He would have said more, but her eyes closed then. He stood there a moment longer, then went out, leaving the tray.

He poked two hundred dollars in notes into Ellen's flour can before dawn the next morning and rode out.

CHAPTER SEVENTEEN

Like blood the years together ran,
his fame and notches grew;
A legend now, no more a man,
the sum of them he slew.

Colorado, July 1870.

John Miller sat a dappled mare under a white-metal sun, watching men string barbed wire and listening to the sweat crackle down his face. When the two men on the ground, heavy shirts soaked through and arms leather-gauntleted to the elbows, finished winding the wire around a cedar post standing four feet out of the caked earth, they stood clear while the man on the driver's seat took the wagon forward, unreeling 150 more yards off the wooden spool in back. Then he hopped off to jack up the left rear wheel while the others clipped the wire free of the spool and wound it around the axle. They spun it taut and a fourth man on horseback rode along the posts and stapled it securely. This done, the process was repeated.

Miller watched about a thousand feet strung before one of the men on the ground held up a hand to halt the operation. He approached the spectator, stripping off his gloves as he came, an inch or two under six feet and maybe 165 pounds of old brown sinew and white handlebars with a fresh scratch on his right cheek that had bled out without his notice. He reached up to take Miller's hand in a hard grip made slippery with sweat. His eyes were a washed-out gray in the brown of his face.

"Good of you to come, Miller. I'm Roy Chessman. Sorry you had to wait, but this here work is still new and it takes time."

"I never knew bobwire was so complicated."

Chessman took off his hat, revealing a full head of startling white hair, and drew a soaked sleeve across his eyes. "Ever damn thing you heard about it is gospel. But I tried every other kind of fence and so far this is the only one that keeps the friendly herds in and the strange herds out. Where do you stand on the subject?"

"Far enough off I don't get cut."

"We shed blood over it sure enough. We got to carry near as much bandage as wire. That ain't the blood I'm concerned about, though. I hope you get on with the stuff. It's what you'll be guarding if you hire on here."

"Who's been cutting it?"

"Riders from that goddamn Triple-T combine east of the Checker C." The Checker C was Chessman's brand, a C linking two squares from a chessboard. "They claim my fence stands in the way of water, but they could drive their damn Herefords north of my spread and get there quicker. They go out of their way to cut my wire. They don't leave one strand up, and there's a month gone replacing it, not even figuring cost."

"You try putting the law on 'em?"

"Well, that's the thing of it. The law gives them the okay to take down any enclosure barring them from water. Mine don't, but I'd have to go to court clear over in Denver to prove it. By then them damn cat-hammed English cows'd have my grass ate down to bare ground and my breeding stock'd be scattered over open range from here to Mexico. Law don't work out here, Miller. You been there, you ought to know that."

"I ain't lawed in three years."

"I heard you deputied in Cripple Creek last year."

"That don't count. I was waiting on a wire from Fort Collins and I needed the posse pay. It lasted two weeks, just long enough to catch the ones held up the mail train outside Denver."

"You killed them was what I heard."

"I killed two. What's stopping you from carrying the fight to this Triple-T outfit?"

"So far no one's got hurt and I aim to keep it that way long as possible. That's how come I sent for you. I need somebody to hold a gun while my men put the fence back up and to patrol it after. You can't string wire one-handed."

"You could have a cowhand do that."

"I got hands riding the survey line now. They can't handle a gun for shit, like every other good man with a rope I ever met. What I want out here is a John Miller. Them combine bastards will think twice when they hear of it."

"I ain't that famous, Mr. Chessman."

"You are around these parts. That Lundgren's store fight got wrote up in every paper in the territory. My four-year-old grandson plays John Miller with the boy from the Q-bar-Q outside church every Sunday."

Miller stretched himself, leaning on his saddle horn. The fence crew was watching them from fifty yards off. "It's kind of tame. I ain't never sat no bobwire before."

"It'll quit being tame in a hot St. Louis minute if your name don't scare them combine men. I don't want no blood, understand. But if it comes to that or my good grass and champion bulls, well, men don't bring what cattle bring on the Denver market. Are you working for me, Mr. Miller?"

"I get free rein out there," the gun man cautioned. "And you back of me when bodies start falling. Comes to a fight, I don't send back no messengers to ask can I start shooting. But we're both of us in it, just as if it's both our hands on the gun."

"Eighty and found. That's twice what I pay my best man, and you won't even have to touch a rope. You sleep in the bunkhouse." The rancher offered his hand a second time.

Miller took it. His face was solemn behind his moustaches. He took business seriously.

The cowhands were difficult to get on with at first. They ran pretty much to his own size—large men were hard on horses—and they appeared not to fear his special skill, but from the moment he first entered the bunkhouse and tossed his bedroll and necessaries onto an unclaimed mattress, he sensed that his presence was alien. They sat on the floor playing with worn pasteboards and wrote letters and read yellowback novels in their bunks by lantern light and didn't acknowledge him, a sure sign that he had aroused their sullen interest.

He made no attempt at conversation. Instead he unrolled the black suit he had bought in Cripple Creek and hung the coat on the peg by his bunk and brushed it, the closest any such wear came to a proper cleaning in that part of the world. He did the same with the trousers and then he rolled the suit back up again tight to keep down the wrinkles and put his canvas bedroll cover on it and used it for a pillow while he stretched out for his first nap on an indoor bed in more than a month. (Chessman's summons had caught up with him across the line in Nebraska.) He knew the others were watching him, expecting him to sleep with one hand on his gun or something, but he disappointed them. He always rested with it tucked under whatever he had for a pillow, where a man could get to it as fast as he would want. His sleep since childhood had lain just on the edge of awakening.

But in time they accepted him, even if they did not grow close. When they rolled out before first light he rose with them, and he ate with them and complained about the food as they did, and when the cook prised the lid off a sugar canister and dropped it cursing when he found a live rattlesnake inside he laughed as loudly as any of them. And before long he was showing them card tricks he had learned from Isham Eagle and telling them about the Lundgren's store fight. In his version all three of the men in the store were armed. He even picked up an idolater in a freckle-spattered young hand called Skid, who followed him everywhere and kept asking him if he knew any of the men he was always reading about in the library of dime novels he kept under his bunk.

Days he accompanied fence crews to the survey lines and sat his horse or worked knots out of his legs while they sank the posts and stretched wire and scrambled cursing out of the way whenever a strand broke loose and lashed around like the tail of a twister, slashing flesh and denim. He helped apply iodine and bandages and entertained them with war stories, after carefully ascertaining who had fought in the war and for what side. The rest of the job had to do with waiting.

Shortly after work started the morning of the fourth day he spotted riders to the east. All morning he watched them coming across featureless plain. The sun was high before they drew close enough for one of Chessman's hands to identify them as Manuel Flores, foreman of the Triple-T, and two of his men. By then Miller, astride his mare, had drawn his new Winchester from its scabbard and levered a cartridge into the chamber. The crisp noise was loud in the outdoor vastness. The three riders held up.

Flores was a surprise, at least half Mexican, with drooping moustaches and long burnsides very black against the smooth oiled wood of his face. He was in his late twenties, a couple of years older than either of the men with him. The three wore the flat-brimmed Stetsons and striped trousers and white bloused shirts that were getting to be the uniform in their work. All had pistols in soft holsters on their hips.

"I ain't seen you before," said Flores. His high, clear voice carried easily across the hundred yards that separated the parties.

"You got that right."

Flores waited for more. Miller rested the carbine across the throat of his saddle and said nothing. The Mexican nodded once. "That wire is against the law. It bars the way to water."

"Mr. Chessman says it don't."

"You one of his cowhands?"

"No."

Flores understood then. He folded his hands atop his saddle horn. "We ain't looking for trouble."

"It ain't something you got to look for. It's lying all over the place waiting."

"My name's Flores."

"John Miller."

If the name meant anything to the foreman he didn't show it. "Miller, this ain't your affair. You never had to cut a friend loose of bobwire and patch him up after. I did, down in New Mexico." It came out "Mesco." So far it was the only word he had trouble saying the American way. "When it ain't cutting up cows and horses and men it cuts up a man's freedom. You don't want to get yourself killed over a few miles of ugly wire."

"Meaning you do."

"Given my way I'd string up the man that invented it with his own wire!"

The vitriolic blast was the first sign of emotion he'd shown. His roan shied, startled. He patted its neck, his eyes on Miller. "Combine won't like hearing Chessman went out and bought himself a gun man."

"Señor Flores, I don't care a nigger's damn what the combine likes and don't like."

"Don't call me señor! My mother was American."

"What'd she tell you your father was?" Miller asked. "Or didn't she know either?"

White teeth flashed in the brown face. Flores gathered his reins. "Mr. Miller, I wouldn't do on a sheep's grave what I'm fixing to do on yours."

He turned his horse and started back the way he'd come, followed momentarily by the others. Miller and the fence crew watched their silhouettes shrink.

"That's a bad man to rile," said one of the hands.

"He did it deliberate!" Young Skid was excited. "He was testing that greaser's limits. Wasn't you, Mr. Miller?"

Miller scabbarded the Winchester. "It's all with them now," he said. "They can pick it up or let it lay."

They finished stringing a half mile with just enough light to get back by. It was Saturday and most of them were talking about town as they went into the bunkhouse to bathe and shave and put on clean clothes. Miller stopped by the pump for a cold drink. He unhooked the tin cup from the nail next to the bunkhouse door and pumped and was bending to catch the water pouring from the spout when a woman came out the back door of the main house across the yard. She had on a yellow bonnet and a matching light shawl in the evening cool and a dress that swept the ground. The light spilling out through the window fell on a delicately rounded face with large eyes and a nose that turned up slightly. She wore a smile that faded gracefully as she slid into the shadows.

"Mr. Miller, you missed."

He stirred himself, looking at Skid, who was pointing to the spout of the pump. The water had finished gushing and Miller had failed to catch a drop of it.

"Here, you hold the cup and I'll pump," offered the young hand.

When the cup was full Miller sipped at it, considering the darkness that had swallowed the woman. "Who was that?"

"Who? Oh, you mean Annie? She's the boss's daughter. She's real nice."

"Her sister the one with the boy? Chessman's grandson?"

"What sister? The grandson's her boy. Only he's away visiting his other grandma and grandpa in Chicago. She's married to Mr. Richardson, the foreman. You met him."

He had—a weathered man nearly Chessman's age. It surprised him. "Don't seem right, an old man like that holding down a high-stepper like her."

"I wouldn't know nothing about that."

Miller looked at the young man, who was blushing in the light from the main house. He wasn't as old as Miller had been when he went to war. The gun man grinned and poured out the rest of his water.

"I tell you about the time I tracked down the leader of the gang robbed the Farmer's Trust in Emporia in '66?"

Skid beamed. "Gosh, no! What happened?"

He returned the cup to its nail. "You introduce me to Mrs. Richardson and I'll tell you the whole story."

CHAPTER EIGHTEEN

Wire and water, they blacken men's souls
and peace is forever forebore;
'Twas Miller it took to tally the toll
in the Gunnison County War.

The first bouquet of wildflowers appeared on the back doorstep of the house Annie Richardson shared with her husband, Hank, on her father's ranch the last Monday morning in July.

It was there when she went out for water to start lunch, a bright yellow spray with dew still on the petals and a bit of twine tied around the stems. She looked around, but the sun was well up and all the hands were out of the nearby bunkhouse and away working. She got the water and poured some in a cut vase that had been a wedding present and arranged the flowers in it and put them on the table for Hank to see when he came home for lunch. He saw them as he was sitting down.

"When'd you find time to pick flowers?" he asked.

She paused with both hands holding up a tray containing a loaf of fresh bread. "I thought they were from you."

"I'm some older than you, but I ain't so old I'd forget doing a thing like that."

"Well, someone did." She set the bread on the table.

"That damn redhead, I bet."

"Rusty? He's over that crush. Besides, he writes poetry."

"Well, if you can write poims you can sure pick flowers." He sawed off a thick slice of bread and smeared butter on it. "I'll talk to him."

"I don't think it was Rusty."

"Whoever it was, he gave some thought to it. Closest them kind of flowers grow is a half-day's ride there and back."

The bouquet wilted quickly and was thrown away. Two days later, another had taken its place, this one twice as big as the first and dotted with red peonies of the sort that grew only along the northern boundary of the Checker C.

"You went out the back door before dawn," Annie told Hank. "Didn't you see them then?"

"They wasn't there then. And Rusty didn't put them there neither. He was with me the whole morning."

"Someone's doing it," she said again.

"I like the way you put things together."

She poured his coffee. "I think it's sweet. Those men are such roughnecks but they're like shy little boys really."

"They're only like that around decent women."

"Oh? You've seen them with the other kind?"

"Not since I hitched up with you, Annie old girl." He slurped soup. "I don't want you taking in no more flowers. Just leave them lay."

"It seems such a shame to let them die."

"Just do like I said. Whoever's doing it will take the hint if he sees them turning brown where he left them."

She touched the petals. "It's only a harmless crush."

"You wouldn't call them harmless if you seen them out there busting steers. Don't take in no more flowers."

A third spray appeared a few days later, more peonies and a single rare prairie rose. She was tempted to take them in anyway and hide them when Hank came for lunch, but it seemed like being unfaithful. She left them there, but she couldn't stop thinking about them. By sundown they had withered and she swept them off the step into the footpath. The next morning, an hour after Hank left to round up some strays across the line in Mesa County, someone knocked on the back door. She opened it and looked at John Miller standing on the step with his hat in one hand and a fresh bouquet in the other.

Hank was gone all day. When she told him about it that night, his face went as white as the streaks in his dark hair. "Don't you talk to that man. He's a common killer."

"He was nice and not at all forward. He said he was too new to the area to have a pretty girl to give flowers to and said he'd be proud if I would accept them."

"I said no more flowers."

"I told him that. He seemed so sad. Oh, Hank, he's just a boy."

"He's older than you. And he's killed better than twenty men."

"I'm sure that's an exaggeration. How many did you kill in the war?"

"That was war. And since when are you so friendly with strangers you ain't been introduced to?"

"Skid introduced us the first week he was here. It was in the yard behind the ranch house when I was on my way to visit with Mama. Skid said, 'Mrs. Richardson, this here is John Miller.' Like he hasn't called me Annie ever since Papa practically adopted him. It was so funny."

"Killers ain't funny. You stay away from him."

She lifted her chin. "I can't have flowers, I can't talk to perfectly civil men who address me in the most gentlemanly terms. You're my husband, not my father!"

"I promised your pa I'd take care of you when I asked him for your hand. That includes protecting you from border trash that gets paid to kill other men. You stay clear of him or I'll send you back to Chicago with little Hank."

She slammed into the bedroom and wept loudly.

The next morning, Miller saw right away that Annie Richardson had told her husband about his visit. The foreman was grumpy and short with the hands struggling to rehang the barn door, and a couple of times he seemed about to address the gun man when he was called away to shout at someone else. Miller, waiting for the fence crew he was guarding that day to arrive, tightened his mare's cinch and said nothing. He had hoped the woman would keep his call a secret, not because he feared an aging cowhand who went around not wearing a gun most of the time, but because it would be a sign his courtship was welcome. Nevertheless he looked forward to the challenge.

He didn't string fence that day after all. Just as the crew was about to leave, Roy Chessman came out of the main house and asked him to accompany Richardson and the buckboard into Gunnison. He explained that his foreman and Manuel Flores of the combine had come to blows the last time they were both in town and if any Triple-T men were there he didn't want them thinking he was hiding his gun man out on the ranch as if he were ashamed of hiring him. Miller said that suited him, he needed a haircut anyway. He had been very conscious of the long hairs curling over his collar when he was with Annie Richardson. Hank clearly loathed the idea of spending any time at all in Miller's company, but he made no protest. Good ranch jobs were scarce enough at his age.

Nor did he get the chance to discuss things with Miller on the way in. Before they cleared the yard, Miller occupying the wagon seat next to Richardson, they were waylaid by the cook, a scraggly-bearded former cowhand with an empty sleeve where a steer horn had claimed his left arm, who needed some supplies he didn't trust to anyone but himself. He climbed up in back and treated his companions to a steady run of tall tales that lasted the entire two hours into Gunnison.

While the cook was in the mercantile and Richardson busied himself loading equipment ordered weeks before through the dry goods, Miller went into the Belle Fleur Saloon, not so much to drink as to get the feel of the town. It was a big room with a clean plank floor and a long glossy cherrywood bar with brass fixtures and two bartenders in white shirts and handlebars. The piano was silent, but at that hour there was already a fair crowd gathered. Voices droned. He found a deserted section of bar, ordered a beer, paid for it, and stood sipping it and studying the room in the long mirror with white-etched borders behind the pulls. After five minutes a man leaned an elbow on the bar next to him, hooking a heel on the brass footrail.

"Mr. Maiden wants to talk to you at his table."

Miller didn't turn to look at him. He could see the man's shiny pink face and crimp-brimmed hat in the mirror. He had blue eyes that twinkled and one of those easy grins that were more habitual than friendly. Out of the corner of his eye Miller noted the smooth hickory handle of a gun with a short barrel curving out through where the man's vest split in front. He drank some more beer. "Just who might Mr. Maiden be and what do I want to talk to him about?"

The grin stayed. The twinkle went. "Mister, when Dick Maiden says he wants to talk to you, you don't ask what about."

Miller finished his beer, not hurrying. He had seen the name Dick Maiden in circus letters on the yellow cardboard covers of several of the dime novels in Skid's collection. He recalled steel engravings of a lean vulpine man with a mane of golden hair and a smoking pistol in each hand. He set down his glass empty and straightened and faced the man at his side for the first time.

"Let's go see the man. I tried working two guns at once one time and I want to ask him how he manages it."

They threaded their way between and around tables, stopping before one in the corner where five men sat holding pasteboards. Stacks of carved wooden checks sorted according to color stood in front of each player. The center of the table was a jumble of them.

The man seated with his back to the corner looked to be in his middle thirties, with dark auburn hair parted in the middle and tumbling in oiled ringlets to his shoulder. His face had a feral look, his slanting eyes and sharp nose and pointed chin making a series of V's that fitted into one another, the whole made oriental by triangles of moustache at the very corners of his mouth. His eyes were yellowish, wolflike. He had on a tailored black Prince Albert over a yellow silk vest with a star pinned to it and a boiled white linen shirt and a black tie knotted carelessly.

For the best part of a minute he watched Miller while smoke twisted up from a long black cheroot burning in a tin ashtray at his elbow. Then he picked it up between a nicotine-stained thumb and forefinger and brought it to his lips. As if this were some kind of signal, the other men at the table scraped back their chairs and got up and walked over to the bar. The grinning man went with them.

"You're Miller," Maiden said. "I saw a cartoon of you in the Emporia paper when I came through there selling hides. You were gone by then."

His voice was deep but smooth, like heavy silk. He gestured with the cheroot at the chair across from him, but Miller moved his head negatively.

"Thanks, I been sitting for two hours."

The yellow eyes came to rest on the revolver in Miller's groin holster. "Remington?"

"Model 1863." Miller moved a hand toward it, then stopped, looking at the other. Maiden nodded and he drew it carefully, giving it a little flip and catching it with his hand around the cylinder to proffer the butt. Accepting it, Maiden swung out the loading gate and turned the cylinder with a thumb to inspect the chambers. "You load it all the way up?" He sounded mildly surprised.

"That about keeping one empty under the hammer is a story. It wouldn't go off if you hit it with a mallet."

"I always figured." He flipped shut the gate and returned the weapon. "I heard the 1863 is no good. The cylinder pin floats around and jams the action."

"No, that's the '61. They fixed that." Miller holstered it.

"This is the best I have found." From the sash around his waist Maiden drew one of a pair of big revolvers with mother-of-pearl grips and gold inlays in the cylinder and offered it butt first. When Miller reached for it, Maiden executed a neat road agent's spin and showed him the muzzle. Miller froze.

Suddenly Maiden smiled, displaying tobacco-dulled teeth, and turned it around again. "Never reach for a pistol with the butt pointed up," he said.

"I'll remember." Miller accepted it. It was a Smith & Wesson, a .44 like his Remington, with a ten-inch barrel and heavy in the muzzle. When he pointed it at an uninhabited section of room it seemed to aim itself.

Maiden said, "It is the American, new this year. The citizens of North Platte presented me with a matched set when I left the sheriff's office there in June."

Miller gave it back, butt down. "I'm still looking for the one that's right for me. Remington comes as close as any so far."

"That is as important as marrying well." Maiden returned the revolver to his sash. "I guess you know I am marshal here. I count it good business to know who is in the area and for what purpose. This affair between Chessman and the combine ranchers is not for town. I have trial enough keeping the peace of a Saturday night without that. I would count it a professional courtesy if you would contain it outside the city limits."

"I hired on to see some wire went up and that it stays up. If it gets to town it won't be me bringing it."

The lawman nodded and picked up his cards. "I place value on a man's word until he demonstrates it to be worthless. I would also thank you to find another saloon to do your drinking in. The Antelope, on the south end of town, waters its whiskey sparingly and offers a free lunch. I don't insist upon it."

By this time the other players, who had been watching from the bar, had returned and were resuming their seats. Dick Maiden put down his cheroot, drew two cards, and threw a fresh check into the pot.

It was a dismissal. Miller's way out led him past the grinning man, who leaned forward and said: "He tell you not to come in here again?"

"He made it a request." Miller looked at him soberly.

"I'm making it good advice."

"Mister, when you figure you earned that right, you come see me."

Miller left the Belle Fleur and crossed the street to the dry goods, where Hank Richardson had finished loading the buckboard and was sitting on the driver's seat smoking a cigarette. The street between the wagon and horse was littered with dead butts. Miller looked up at him.

"I just met Marshal Maiden."

The foreman flipped the stub away to join the others. "He say anything?"

"He drawed a line and said let's each keep to his own side."

"He's just waiting to see which way the wind's blowing before he spits."

Miller watched Richardson draw the makings from his shirt pocket and roll another cigarette. "There something you wanted to talk to me about?"

"I been studying on it."

"Well?"

He licked the paper. "Not yet."

The gun man nodded noncommittally. "Well, if you feel the need in the next half hour or so you'll find me getting my hair cut."

"Go on ahead. Cook'll be that long arguing over the price of dried apples."

The barbershop was clean and sunny and smelled of lime water and cut hair. Miller watched the small, natty barber scrape the last of the lather off a fat townsman wearing a ruby ring on his right little finger and then took his place in a brown leather chair rubbed shiny by an army of patient backsides. Tying the sheet behind his customer's neck to protect his town suit, the barber said:

"You're John Miller. I saw the way you wear your pistol and I said to myself, 'That man lives with his gun.' Yessir, I spotted that right off. I'm a student of people and their occupations. I look at them and

I guess right a hundred times out of a hundred. I could've been a Pinkerton, but my father wanted me to be a professional man. Bet yours wanted the very same thing."

"I can't say. He got kicked to death by a mule before he had the chance to tell me."

Scissors clicked. "I started out to be a doctor, but the sight of blood disquieted me. I guess that's why I'm such a good barber. *Ha*-ha. What sort of cut would you like?"

"A quiet one."

Two men in cowboy dress entered the shop a few minutes later. The barber glanced up and said, "Be with you right away, Mr. Flores. Have yourself a seat. That's this month's *Harper's* there on the table; just came in this morning."

"You're out of bay rum, Sid," said the Triple-T foreman. His eyes were on Miller, looking back at him from the chair with the sheet spread over him from knees to chin.

"No, there's a brand-new bottle right there on that shelf next to you." The barber pointed with his scissors.

Flores unstopped the bottle and upended it over the steel basin. It gulped empty after a few seconds. He replaced it on the shelf.

Sid opened his mouth, then closed it. He laid down the scissors and took off his apron. "I need some more bay rum," he muttered, and went out past the two men. He pulled the door shut behind him.

Flores hadn't looked at him once, or at anything but the man in the chair. The Triple-T foreman said, "You should of stayed behind your wire," and pulled a Colt's Peacemaker out of the soft holster on his hip.

The room throbbed then; fire erupted from the sheet covering Miller, and a line of ceramic and cut-glass bottles exploded within a foot of Flores' right arm. He jumped, his dark eyes rattling.

The sheet smoldered where Miller's Remington had blasted a hole through it. Bits of burning jute swirled like fireflies in the smoky air. He swept aside the sheet with his left hand.

"Lay it down, Señor Flores," he said. "In the basin."

The foreman was slow to obey. His right sleeve and pants leg were soaked and the atmosphere was thick with spent powder and lilacs. Finally he inserted the long barrel inside the lip of the basin and let the Colt's slide to the bottom. He raised his hands.

Miller moved his eyes to Flores' companion, a big man for a cow-hand, with a stone jaw and bright eyes that seemed vaguely familiar despite a ragged set of moustaches. He turned his palms outward slowly. He was unarmed.

Watching him, Miller felt his lips part.

"Howdy, Gene," the cowhand said. "I reckon you're answering quicker to John these days."

The foreman looked from Miller to the man at his own side. "You know him?"

The cowhand said, "He's my brother."

CHAPTER NINETEEN

Brother fight brother, swept up in a flood,
and cattle the spoils of the game;
Two strangers related in birth by their blood,
separated in death by the same.

"Matt said you was bigger than him," Miller told Jerome. "I didn't credit it."

"It's hell on finding cow work. I'd just as soon it was me took after Ma's side instead of you."

They were drinking at a corner table in the Antelope, a saloon with much simpler appointments than the elegant Belle Fleur, but the drinks were cheaper and the beer seemed cooler. Actually, the big lump of ice that the redheaded bartender stirred ostentatiously around inside the open barrel was solid glass. The pronghorn head that gave the establishment its name decorated a cedar wall whose stained surface bore evidence of past attempts to spit tobacco into the trophy's marble eyes.

"Flores is no better or worse than any other cowman I worked under," Jerome said. "He's mean, but he's loyal to them that pay him."

Miller had allowed the Triple-T foreman to ride home, with the understanding that he could reclaim his revolver at the barbershop next visit. When Jerome told Flores he'd meet him at the ranch later, he snarled something in Spanish and left.

Miller said, "According to Matt, you went down Texas way to become a cattle baron."

"I was doing okay too, till the goddamn Comanches stole all my horses and run off the herd I had started. I come back from town to find my partner strung upside down from a cottonwood over a dead fire. Your skull don't really burst from that, I found out; it just kind of cooks. Anyway, I buried him and hired on with the first drive heading north. Been living off other men's beeves ever since."

"It's a hard life."

"They're all of them hard out here."

"Ma's in a bad way," said Miller, after a pause. "Or she was when I seen her last, a time back. Could be she's dead by now."

Jerome hesitated with his glass halfway to his lips. Then he raised it the rest of the way and drank and set it down. "Ain't a lot I can do to change that, I reckon. Matt, he can take care of things."

"He's married now, Matt is. Got him a son."

"He always was the one for lighting someplace permanent." The younger Morner flicked foam off his moustaches. "It'd been different if Maureen didn't die. Living there was dark after that. Ma, she went to bed thirty-six one night and got up sixty the next morning. Matt's stronger than me. He stuck. I got out first chance."

"I hear you fought for the North."

"I hear you fought for yourself. Way I hear it you still are. You're commencing to cast a long shadow in this country."

Miller changed the subject. "What's the combine?"

"New York railroad muckety named Trainor and an Englishman— Lord Taunton or something on that order—and this John Trench that runs the show. Colonel Trench, he's called. I had a nickel for every man that come out of that war a colonel I wouldn't be working for wages. He's the only one spends any time here." He smiled the tight, tormented farmer's smile that reminded Miller of their father. "Looks like you and me are enemies."

"These range wars never amount to much."

"Well, maybe." Jerome had some more beer.

"Maybe means what?"

"Well, hell, you're my brother. There's some hard asses been show-ing up in the chow line the last few days. Roundup's winding down so I can't think why the Colonel's hiring, and anyway these don't smell like your everyday cowhands."

"How many?"

"Four or five."

"They can't all be guns. Nobody's rich enough to salary that many new men just to hang around waiting for trouble to start. Any names?"

"Just one I heard. Alan or Albert something. Lawhorn, that's it."

"Alvin Lawhorn?"

"Alvin, yeah. You know him?"

"I heard of him. He was mixed up in that MacPhail-Bishop thing up Cheyenne way last year. He's no more cowhand than I am."

"My thinking is his work's through when you're in the ground."

The conversation fell off after that, and Miller was relieved when Hank Richardson entered the saloon, spotted them, and approached their table.

"They said at the barbershop you was here," he told Miller. "We got to get started we want to be back by dark."

Miller drained his glass and stood. "I'm obliged, Jerome."

"Family's family. Just forget where you heard it."

"For a stranger in town you sure make friends fast," commented Richardson on their way back to the buckboard.

Miller said, "This one and me go back some."

"Chessman won't like that, you cuddling up to one of them combine men."

"It ain't Chessman you're worried about, and it ain't a combine man you're worried about me cuddling up to."

Richardson stopped and faced him. They had stepped off the boardwalk and were in the street. The foreman's seamed face was dark as old blood.

"You stay away from my house and let my wife be. I don't know nor care how many other men's wives you stole. You let this one be."

"You talk to her?"

"There ain't no her where you're concerned."

"Could be she thinks different."

"Mister, you ain't listening."

"You don't want to fight me, Hank."

The foreman straightened, emphasizing the inch of height he had on Miller. "Roy Chessman and me fit the Mexicans and the Comanches and the southern Cheyennes for this here country when Gunnison was just a shady rock for rattlers and scorpions to crawl under out of the sun. Before that I was knocking down men in a Virginny coalyard when you was still learning how to say Daddy. You think I'm afeared of you and that pistol?"

"If I didn't, it'd be because I thought you was dumber than I know you are."

Something moved under Richardson's face then. "You just let Annie be." He resumed walking.

The cook supplied most of the conversation on the way back to the Checker C, complaining about what civilization was doing to the price of flour. The buttes to the north were red in the westering sun. August was well along, with the scent of autumn coming down from Montana and Wyoming.

A horseman hailed them just inside the ranch gate. As he came cantering toward them across flat plain, Miller lifted his Winchester out of the box behind the seat and racked in a cartridge. Richardson touched the gun man's arm. "It's Chessman."

The rancher's face was all pulled-down lines and shadow. "Where'd they hit?" demanded his foreman before he said anything.

"Northwest corner. Man with the words kept Nate Osborne busy talking while the rest opened fire. Nate was the last one hit. Then they cut the wire and rode off."

"Anyone killed?"

"Skid's the only one made it back."

"Jesus!"

"He took one clean through both cheeks. They left him for killed but he got a seat and rode back. I don't know how he managed to say as much as he did before he passed out. I sent Rusty Smith into town for the doc. You didn't pass him?"

"He must of rid cross-country. Who'd we lose besides Nate?"

"Rudy Lenz and Fat Jack."

"Aw," said the cook. "Aw, not Jack."

Miller said, "It wasn't Manuel Flores. I seen him in town."

"Skid didn't know any of 'em."

"Alvin Lawhorn."

Chessman looked hard at Miller.

"Something I heard in town," he explained. "Combine's hired on some soldiers of its own. We can hit them tonight. They won't be expecting it before morning."

"No, I don't want any of my men riding on Triple-T property at night. They'll be shot for rustlers and it'll be my word against Colonel Trench's. Trench owns the sheriff."

"He don't own Dick Maiden."

"This ain't Maiden's jurisdiction. Anyway, I don't trust him to throw in with us. We'll pay the Colonel a dawn visit. Skid gave me a fair description of the man that did all the talking. I want to see is he there. If he is I'll swear out a complaint. The sheriff'll have to arrest him just for looks. If Skid identifies him we can get a U.S. marshal in here and settle this thing."

"What if Skid dies?" Richardson asked.

"Then we kill everything with a Triple-T brand on it and hang for wolves." The rancher gathered his reins. "Let's go. We got bodies to bring back before we lose the light."

The party that left the Checker C at dawn the next day consisted of Roy Chessman, Hank Richardson, John Miller, and two hands named Harry and Dave, veterans of the late war. The men wore pistols and carried rifles in saddle scabbards or slung from butt rings, more weight than most of them had carried in years. Their saddles and bridles creaked in the cool air of morning.

Combine headquarters stood a mile inside the gate leading on to the Triple-T Ranch. Miller was surprised to learn that the building was no larger than Chessman's own home. Considerably more money and effort had been spent on the whitewashed barn nearby. As they approached the long porch on horseback, the only living thing in sight was a shedding goat busy gnawing at the rawhide tether securing it to the pump in the front yard.

"Well, I don't much like *this,*" Richardson told Chessman.

"Roy, you're trespassing."

They looked up at an open window on the second story, where a man with a full gray beard stood in a stiff white shirt with no collar and black suspenders.

Chessman said, "Not technically. I ain't been asked to leave."

"I suppose you know there are six guns trained on you at this moment."

Miller had spotted two of them, a rifle barrel sticking out of a mound of hay in the open door to the barn loft and metal glinting in red sunlight behind one of the windows on the ground floor of the house.

"Colonel, I didn't get to be older than you being stupid," Chessman replied. "But I'd admire to know how come you're so unhospitable."

"Word gets around. I heard about your trouble yesterday. It was inevitable you'd blame the combine, even though no one from the Triple-T went anywhere near your property all day."

"Then I reckon it was the wind shot my men and cut my wire."

"I am not the only man in the territory who is opposed to barbed wire. Furthermore the law stands with me. I need not go outside it."

"I got a man says different."

They could hear the goat chomping rawhide in the silence that dropped down on the end of Chessman's statement. He went on.

"Your boys got careless, Colonel. They didn't finish the job."

Colonel Trench chuckled quietly. It was a deep, hollow sound, like earth striking the lid of a coffin.

"You amuse me. I was a lawyer before the war. Nonexistent eyewitnesses are a courtroom staple."

"You got a man working for you calls himself Alvin Lawhorn," Chessman said. "We're here to get a look at him."

"I hire men to work, not place themselves on public display. If you wish to visit with one of my hands, come back at the end of the ranch day. Alone."

"I'm Lawhorn."

Heads turned toward the barn loft, where the man at the other end of the rifle stood up and brushed hay off his trousers with his free hand. Hatless, he wore his brown hair parted in the middle and pomaded into upswept wings on either side and a darker beard trimmed close to his chin. A slight paunch strained at his gun belt. His rifle was a Remington rolling-block with a folding sight, beloved of buffalo runners and army snipers. As he rose, Dave lifted the Henry he'd unslung from his saddle ring as they'd entered the ranch. Richardson reached out and clamped strong fingers on the man's arm, halting him. "You want to get us cut to pieces?"

Chessman said, "Your man's too big and heavy for cow work, Colonel. Maybe you got him shoveling shit."

"Maybe you want to lie under it," Lawhorn returned.

"Easy." Colonel Trench hadn't stirred at his window. He held himself as erect as a military statue. "State your business, Roy. Whom I hire and for what purpose is not it."

Chessman was silent for a long minute. Then he backed up his gray.

"We're done here. I'm obliged for the look. Next visit we bring the sheriff with a warrant for Lawhorn's arrest."

"Do you really believe the word of an ignorant cowhand will stand up in court?"

"That's up to the court. You have yourself a good day, Colonel. Boys, let's not take up any more of the man's time."

Miller was the last to join the procession. He had held back to commit Alvin Lawhorn's figure and features to memory, and by the way the man had stared steadily back it was apparent he was doing the same. Miller felt the Remington between his shoulder blades for half a mile. The rifle had a phenomenal range.

Harry spurred ahead to ride abreast of his employer. "Mr. Chessman, I was there when Skid described the man that did all the talking when him and the rest was shot. What he said didn't fit this Lawhorn at all."

"We know that, but Trench and Lawhorn didn't. He was there all right. The Colonel just told us that."

"What now?" demanded Richardson.

Chessman said, "That's up to Skid and the Lord."

A few days later, Skid died of blood poisoning without regaining consciousness.

CHAPTER TWENTY

A dying art, the gun man's skill,
but greatly in demand;
If you've a man in mind to kill,
depend you on his hand.

The last survivor of the raid on the Triple-T died in 1936 at seventy-two of viral pneumonia while visiting her granddaughter and her granddaughter's husband in Seattle. The child of a cowhand and the Mexican cook, she was six years old and playing in the front yard when the battle broke out. Her account of it up to the point where a stray bullet smashed her left hand (which had to be removed later) is the basis for most of the histories that followed.

The number of men in the raiding party varies according to the account, but most agree that it included Chessman, Richardson, Rusty Smith, and that same Harry and Dave who were present on the first visit, and whose surnames are lost to history. The small number of casualties is astonishing in view of the estimated two hundred bullets fired and that the raiders caught the combine men as they were returning to the bunkhouse for lunch. Three Triple-T men died, one a former lieutenant of Bloody Bill Anderson's and almost certainly a member of the band that wiped out the Checker C fence crew some ten days earlier; eight were wounded including Manuel Flores, two Chessman hands were killed, and Chessman himself lost most of the use of his right arm when a .45 ball tore through his shoulder. The shooting continued sporadically for seven hours from the cover of various outbuildings and ended with dusk, when the raiders rode away. Among those buried were Rusty Smith and Hank Richardson.

John Miller was not present during the fight. He was in Gunnison, engaged in a running gun battle with Alvin Lawhorn and an unidentified gun man said to be in Colonel Trench's employ. Miller had been dispatched to town almost at the last minute, when word came from a combine man friendly to the Checker C that Lawhorn had gone to town. The informant was believed to be Miller's brother Jerome Morner, found shot to death a month later on the Triple-T range by an unknown assailant. Miller received a thigh wound and Lawhorn lived for twenty-eight days with bullet fragments in both lungs before pneumonia took him. He's buried in the old town cemetery with the legend "MURDERED BY KILLER MILLER SEPTEMBER 11, 1870" chiseled on his stone, although most of it has been chipped away by souvenir hunters. It is not known what became of his partner.

The same doctor who had treated Skid removed the bullet from Miller's leg, cleaned and dressed the wound, and had him taken to the hotel, where his room was charged to Chessman. The gun man received three visitors during his stay. The first was Marshal Dick Maiden.

"We had an agreement," the lawman told him sadly. "You would not bring the trouble to town and I would not ask you to leave."

"Sometimes agreements don't work out." Miller lay in a nightshirt borrowed from the doctor with his bandaged leg elevated on a pile of pillows. Sections of the county newspaper's extra edition detailing the violence in town and at the Triple-T littered the floor next to the bed.

Maiden maneuvered to place a windowless corner at his back. The scarlet sash around his middle with the white mother-of-pearl gun handles showing above it put the wounded man in mind of a shaving cut in fresh lather. "That friend of Lawhorn's must have left town. I would send out wires, but I don't want him back. Lawhorn is doing me the good grace of dying, though I would have him do it quicker."

His amber wolf's-gaze left Miller in no doubt about the progression of his thoughts. The gun man said, "I never been known for my good grace. Doc says I'll live."

"I prescribe a speedy recovery and a fast horse. The Colonel's men are something to see when the burying fever is upon them. They won't want to stop once their own are in the ground."

"They'll wait for Colonel Trench to get back from Denver first. He'd been home when this all happened, the war would be finished."

"Not as long as there was a combine man left to go on hating."

The marshal grasped the doorknob. "Soon as you can trust that leg I want you to keep using it until you're over the line."

Roy Chessman came in a few days later. The rancher had on a black suit freshly brushed and his right arm was in a white sling. Miller took a second recognizing him. He looked like one of those old men one saw around town. With his left hand Chessman drew a thick envelope from inside his coat and placed it on the nightstand next to the bed.

"There's two months' wages there and a hunnert-dollar bonus for taking out Lawhorn," he said. "You can appreciate I can't afford to go on paying cowhand's wages to someone who don't do cow work now that the thing's done."

Miller said, "I didn't know it was done."

"Governor's asked the U.S. Marshal's office to send men into the county and see it gets done. We don't lose, the Triple-T don't lose. We don't neither of us win, neither. I just seen Smith and Hank Richardson put under."

"Sorry about Richardson."

"Hank and I stood off sixty Cheyennes for three days and nights in a dugout with a dozen cartridges between us. We raised us some hell them times." The glitter of memory died in the washed-out eyes. "My grandson gets in from Chicago on Saturday's train. I got to tell him his mother's a widow."

"How is she?"

"She's a Chessman. She's out in the hall now. She wants to talk to you."

That surprised Miller. "What about?"

"She won't say. I'll be outside." The rancher opened the door. "I won't see you again."

"You been white to me, Mr. Chessman. I don't get that very much."

"I wish to hell I never seen you."

He went out. Annie Richardson entered a moment later. She was dressed in black from head to foot, her features blurred behind a thick veil. Her hands were hidden in the folds of her skirt.

"Mrs. Richardson—"

She lifted a gloved right hand with a short pistol in it. "You killed Hank."

He put his hands behind his back, bracing himself against the headboard. His gun belt hung on the post with the Remington in its holster. It was a two-foot reach and her finger was on the pocket gun's trigger. "It was combine men done that," he said. "I wasn't even there."

"Hank was a married man. He wouldn't take a chance with his life unless he thought he had something to prove. We both killed him. But he'd still be alive if it weren't for you." She drew back the hammer with both thumbs.

He threw a pillow at her. She flinched. Fire leaped, the air was swallowed in a roar, a clump of feathers burst apart and fluttered all over the room like tiny birds set free. The woman staggered and Miller lunged and scooped the .44 Remington out of its sheath. The movement sent white heat through his injured thigh. The door exploded open and Roy Chessman slung out a long arm with a foot and a half of Colt Peacemaker at the end of it, the bore as big as the room for the man on the other end. The rancher's other arm was around the woman, sobbing uncontrollably now with the small pistol dangling forgotten from one hand. The scene resembled an advertisement for a morality play.

"Drawing down on women now, Mr. Miller?"

The gun man sat with his good leg doubled under him and the Remington covering both his visitors. "Only on them that draw down on me first."

Chessman slanted his Colt upward and let down the hammer.

"Get well quick," he said. "And get out."

Alone again minutes later, holding his throbbing wound, Miller reflected that he had been in friendlier towns.

"Mr. Miller?"

"Who's asking?"

The stranger handed him a card:

CURTIS STACKABLE

CONTEMPORARY HISTORIAN

Miller looked his visitor over a second time. It was another hotel room in another town, this time in Wyoming, and the gun man was wearing his town suit. Except during rainstorms and blizzards, the

wound in his thigh hadn't bothered him in more than two years. The
man in the hallway was two inches taller than he in a loose-fitting suit
with a tiny black-and-white check that appeared to float if one stared
at it long enough. He wore his black hair collar length and brushed
straight back from an even line across his forehead. His beard was
trimmed to conform to a square jaw and he had bright eyes that
barely flickered at the sight of the revolver Miller was holding.

"What's a contemporary historian?"

"May I?" Stackable put his free hand on the briefcase he carried
under one arm.

Miller moved his head. The clasp came open and the bearded
dandy pulled out four books bound in yellow cardboard. Seeing that
there were no weapons in the briefcase, Miller leathered the Schofield
.45 he had begun carrying that year and accepted the books.

They were like the ones Skid used to collect at the Checker C, with
action engravings on the covers and skirling titles made out of gun-
smoke. Each of the four bore the name of a different author. "All of
these contemporary historians?"

"They are. Or rather, he is. I wrote all of these books, and eighty
more besides."

"You ashamed of it?"

"No, it's just that I write them so fast this is the only way my
publishers have of keeping track of sales."

Miller paged through one, stopping here and there to look at illus-
trations. "I was in Colorado Springs when this happened," he said,
indicating one that showed a man with a bowie knife holding at bay a
roomful of men with guns. "It was Jed Menick against three men, not
ten. And he was the only man armed, and that with a scattergun."

"I wrote it the way it was told to me by Mr. Menick. Since he was
the lone survivor I had no choice but to set it down as related. That's
why I am here, Mr. Miller; to hear the unvarnished side of things."

"Speak plain, Mr. Stackable."

The writer's eyes glittered. "Why should a man like Jed Menick,
who by your own testimony is a flummerer, be held aloft as a frontier
hero while the genuine article goes unsung? Readers in Chicago know
of your exploits through the journals. Farther east they are ignorant of
your very existence, yet they clamor for more stories from the border.
Will you consent to an interview?"

The gun man couldn't believe it. "You know what's going on?"

"Well, I heard Joe Ayers has issued a challenge and that he expects you to meet him out in the street in about an hour. That's why I thought you might consider talking to me."

"Meaning while I'm still breathing." He returned the books.

"Not at all, sir. I reasoned merely that you might welcome the opportunity to make the time pass more quickly while setting the record straight, as it were."

"You're a sore liar, Mr. Stackable. If you thought me likely to win this one you'd be talking to Ayers and count on selling every copy as the last interview with a dead man."

"Sir, it's 1873. Man-killers of your description seem part of the late war. I have come out in search of them with small success and it is only by chance that we are both in Laramie on the same day. I assure you the thought—"

"It's all right. I ain't complaining. Fact, I'd do the same thing in your place. Step inside."

He sat his guest down in the room's only chair and offered him a tilt from the bottle he had bought in Cheyenne—it was declined—and talked until the hour was almost up, prodded on by questions fired almost as fast as the writer's hand racing across the pages of his pocket notebook. He began with his father's death, revealing his own birth name for the first time publicly, told of his fight with Curly and the Cheyenne he killed on the way to Missouri and shaded his war experiences a little and set forth the fight at Lundgren's store in Emporia as a battle of the law against evil whiskey traders and held pretty much to the line on the Gunnison County War, leaving out only Annie Richardson. By then Joe Ayers was calling for him out in the street. He let the window curtain slide back and rammed the cork into the bottle, stamping a period on the end of the epic.

"That brings us to 1870," Stackable said, writing furiously. "What of the last three years?"

"Drifting, mostly, picking up piecework here and there. I helped bust up a miners' strike in Creede last year, and that was my steadiest work since Gunnison. You never know when you're going to eat next in this work, so when you do you stuff yourself."

"Like a wolf."

"Well, there's a place for wolves too."

Stackable rose and returned his writing materials to his briefcase. He had filled one notebook and half of a second. "I forgot to ask. What is Ayers' argument with you?"

"I shot his brother or something. I disremember the details." Miller ran his revolver sideways up his shirtsleeve. The cylinder ratcheted.

"Good luck, Mr. Miller."

The gun man took the hand offered. "I'll be reading the book for mistakes."

When the writer left, Miller slipped into his suitcoat, peering through the net curtain at Joe Ayers' thick figure shielding his eyes against the sun to look up at Miller's window. Quietly the gun man let himself out.

In the hallway he drew a key from his pocket, walked down to the end by the stairs, and used it to unlock the door to the corner room. Inside he lifted his Winchester off the bed without bothering to work the lever. A cartridge already rested in the chamber.

The window was open in spite of the early November chill. Through it he saw Ayers down the block, raising cupped hands to his mouth.

"Miller, you coming out or—"

The cracking report bounded off the false fronts of the buildings on both sides of the street. Ayers spun on his heel and flopped down on his shoulder, raising a swell of dust that dissipated quickly in the wind. He kicked twice, arched his back, and settled while the echo was still growling.

On the ground floor of the hotel, the dapper clerk and Curtis Stackable witnessed the death through the front window. As the body subsided, the clerk said: "I asked him why a man would want to rent two rooms when he could only sleep in one at a time."

"What did he say?" The notebook was out.

The clerk watched a crowd forming around the corpse. "He said he never does his shooting and his sleeping in the same place."

The package caught up with him in Casper around Christmas 1874, about the time he was deciding for reasons of health not to throw in with either side in the Kettleman Feud. It was paving-stone-shaped, although not nearly so heavy, and wrapped in brown paper so ragged and travel-stained the return address was illegible. He tore it free and looked at a fair image of himself rendered in black ink on dull yellow with a revolver in each hand.

HELL ON THE FRONTIER
Being a Factual Account of the
Life and Stirring Adventures
of
John "Killer" Miller
In His Own Words
as told to
Will Lockhammer

When he opened the stiff cover, a sheet of paper folded in thirds fell out. He picked it up and unfolded it. The script was bold and unhesitant, rendered by a hand accustomed to holding a pen.

Dear Mr. Miller:

I have attempted as closely as possible to set down the events of your life as you related them to me. However, because of the book's required length and the necessary brevity of our interview, I was forced to draw from the files of newspapers in Missouri, Kansas, and Colorado to flesh out the remaining pages. I earnestly hope you will not take offense at this.

You will be pleased to know that the book has enjoyed a lively sale in the few weeks it has been out; so much so, in fact, that the publisher has asked me to invite you to come to Chicago as his guest, for conversations with the press and more detailed interviews in preparation for the next book about John Miller.

If you are interested, please wire me in care of:

Popular Publications, Inc.
1670 North Michigan Avenue
Chicago, Illinois

Please tell me your location, and a train ticket will be immediately forthcoming.

With gratitude, and hoping to hear from you soon, I am

Yours most sincerely,

Curtis Stackable

"Will Lockhammer," et al.

CHAPTER TWENTY-ONE

It ain't so true now, the world turns around,
but in them days they said it was so;
While some men may finish in holes in the ground,
the rest of them go to Chicago.

John Miller was coming hard on thirty-three the day his train pulled
into the city of Chicago, and there were times, feeling his muscles
lock while lying wrapped in a thin blanket under a December sky or
reading a newspaper account of the exploits of some nineteen-year-old
killer out in Nevada, when he felt ninety. But from his first glimpse of
the spired plain of buildings under a dirty-gray umbrella of anthracite
smoke, he had felt thirteen again, an Iowa boy on his first visit to St.
Louis. However, the Gateway to the West was just a village of hovels
compared to this fearsome great crawling beast of wood and brick and
black macadam. He feared no man, but hordes unsettled him, and he
had not seen so many people in his life all told as he saw in the
minutes between the time the train entered the city's outskirts and
when it whooshed and shrieked to a stop alongside a wooden platform
carpeted with strangers. A mob of such proportions needn't lynch a
man; it could tear him to pieces in seconds. While his fellow passen-
gers were lining up in the aisle, he transferred his Schofield revolver
from his valise to the deep leather pocket he had had tailored into his
suitcoat for that purpose. Only then did he take his place in the
procession.

"Mr. Miller! Here!"

Before he spotted his features, he recognized Curtis Stackable's
checked suit under a black overcoat flapping open in the jostling
crowd of arrivals, departures, greeters, and train-watchers. Using his
valise as a pry bar, Miller worked his way through the press of bodies

until he stood before the writer. Stackable shook his hand and took his bag and introduced him to his companion, a tall thin white-haired man with a spade-shaped beard and a tweed Chesterfield buttoned so high only the silken knot of his purple cravat showed. He had on a pearl gray derby that brought memories of Ben Honey and his name was Winthrop Leland, president and general manager of Popular Publications, Inc. Miller grasped a dry skeletal hand that seemed cold even for February on Lake Michigan.

"No topcoat, Mr. Miller?" observed the publisher, in a surprisingly youthful falsetto. "You must be freezing."

"No, I just can't feature wearing one in this here warm eastern weather."

The Chicagoans laughed politely at this example of frontier humor. In fact, Miller had sold his good buffalo coat and his old Winchester to pay for the new suit. His employment had suffered a long dry spell since Laramie.

He was escorted to a waiting four-wheeler, where he sat with his back to the driver and tried not to shiver in the icy wind while Stackable informed him of his itinerary.

"We have arranged a press meeting at the office for this afternoon," began the writer. "The reporters wanted to meet your train but we restrained them, thinking you'd rather rest at the hotel first. Afterward we have reservations at one of Chicago's finest restaurants and tickets to the theater later. How do you find the city so far?"

"Too damn crowded."

They checked him into the Palmer House, where a clerk with his hair slicked back like an otter's coat fluttered about and rang for a boy in a tight coat with brass buttons to carry his valise up to a suite done in burgundy and green plush. Pledging to return for him at four o'clock, Leland and Stackable left him in the lobby. Alone in the suite a few minutes later, he hung up his suit, laid out a second layer of long underwear for his next outside expedition, placed his pistol on the nightstand, and stretched out on the featherbed to look at the ceiling and tote up the number of hotel rooms he had stayed in since leaving the Missouri Militia. He fell asleep at thirty.

A knock at the outside door awoke him after an hour. Thinking it was his hosts come to collect him, he walked through the parlor and opened it in his underwear, having paused to pick up the Schofield just in case. A handsome red-haired woman in blue satin fastened to the throat flickered green eyes over him from head to foot and smiled.

"Mr. Stackable invited me," she said.

After a second he grinned and put away the revolver. Stackable had even thought to pick one several inches shorter than the gun man.

The publishing offices occupied two floors of an eleven-story building on North Michigan Avenue. The reception area, under the command of a woman in her forties with pince-nez eyeglasses on a black cord and a white blouse without ruffles, displayed that month's covers behind glass and a photographic portrait of Winthrop Leland in a Yankee major's uniform standing next to a cadaverous Abraham Lincoln. Stackable ushered Miller down an aisle lined with starched female typists seated at black-and-gold Remington writing machines and into a room with two rows of folding chairs and no one sitting in any of them. Instead, a dozen men in derbies and overcoats and twelve different varieties of facial hair stood around with their hands in their pockets, talking in nasal voices like geese yapping in a pen. In the room's heat, their heavy woolens gave off an oppressive stench not unlike urine.

At sight of Miller, looking slim and not short in his well-cut frock coat and white linen and new Stetson, they subsided into silence. Stackable raised his hands unnecessarily, a conductor summoning the attention of an already rapt orchestra, made a short introduction, and started the questioning with the craggy bearded correspondent from the *Times*.

"How many men have you killed?"

"None that weren't out to kill me," Miller said.

"I mean the proper number."

"Ten or eleven."

"Your book says that by the time you were twenty-one you'd killed a man for every year of your life."

"I reckon I should of read it or I'd know."

The reporters made amused snorts and scribbled in their notebooks. "What do you think of Dick Maiden getting shot down in Tucson?" asked the young man from the *Tribune*, Miller's height but forty pounds heavier.

"He wore the star too long."

"I heard it was over a woman," someone said.

The *Times* man said, "I want to clear up this business of the men you've killed. There was the fellow on the wagon train, and the Cheyenne warrior, and five anyway during the war, and that Arkansas nigger-killer Gunderson, and Fick Wilson and Otto Lundgren at the store, and Alvin Lawhorn, and this man Ayers in Laramie year before last. That's twelve right there."

"I had help with some of them," replied Miller. "Anyway, it ain't Christian to count."

"We've heard some dastardly things here about Charley Slaughter," said a cat-whiskered man who introduced himself as a contributor to the *Chicago Detective Quarterly*. "What sort of man was he?"

"If not for Major Fouché I wouldn't be standing here. He taught me most of what I know about guerrilla fighting."

"What's to know? Get behind a man and gun him down."

Miller looked flatly at the man from the *Times*. "What do you know about it till you been there?"

"Is it true you and Fick Wilson were interested in the same woman?" The *Tribune*.

"What's between me and a lady stays that way."

"Was Alvin Lawhorn faster than you?" The *Sun*—olive skin, beard a vertical black bar.

"Why don't you go dig him up and ask him?"

"Is Isham Eagle faster than you?" The *Detective Quarterly*.

"No. He ain't fast at all. But he taught me the rest of what I needed to know."

"Isham Eagle not fast? Come on."

"Speed's got nothing to do with it. Graveyard's full of fast men. Pick your target and take your time and you'll come through ninety-nine times out of a hundred."

"What about the hundredth?" The *Times* man's smile was nasty in his beard.

"Well, what's twelve from a hundred? That's as many as I got left before I find out."

"Are you going to see Eagle while you're in town?" The *Sun*.

"Ish is in Chicago?" He was looking at Stackable, who nodded.

"He's appearing at Nixon's Amphitheater. Those are the tickets I mentioned. It was going to be a surprise."

"Well, it still is."

"Going to talk over old crimes?"

Miller turned his full attention on the man from the *Times*, who had stopped writing in his notebook. Before he could respond, Winthrop Leland's piping voice cut through the atmosphere. The white-bearded publisher had slipped into the room unnoticed.

"Gentlemen, this inquisition is through. Mr. Miller has just arrived in town. There will be many other opportunities to speak with him. Thank you all for coming, and please remember to mention Popular Publications and *Hell on the Frontier* in your stories."

The *Times* man was last to leave, fixing his nasty smile on Miller before he turned and followed his colleagues out.

"He didn't take to me at all," observed the gun man.

Stackable said, "He's from Kansas originally. His sister was killed by night riders during the war. We were hoping his paper would send someone else."

Beaming parentally, Leland changed the subject. "How long has it been since you and Eagle saw each other?"

"Not since Emporia," said Miller.

Stackable tugged down the points of his vest. "You will find him changed, I think."

He Rode with Slaughter!
He Fought at Lundgren's Store!
ISHAM EAGLE,
Last Hereditary Chief
of the Dread Cherokee Tribe
of Savage Indians,
Lectures TONIGHT
His Subject:
LIFE ON THE SCOUT
A Rousing Reminiscence of Adventures in the Great West
and an Edifying Experience for our Impressionable Youth!
Ladies Also Welcome

The card, printed in circus characters, stood three feet high on an easel just inside the theater entrance. Miller read it and grunted.

"He's chief of the Cherokees like I'm Emperor of Mexico. I wonder who put him on to that."

"Our rivals, the Dime Press." Towering in his silk hat and caped overcoat, Leland was the only one of the three in evening dress; Miller wore his new suit with the revolver in its special pocket and Curtis Stackable had on his ubiquitous check. "They published Eagle's memoirs as a morality tract with something less than success. Now they seek to play off yours. The fight at Lundgren's store indeed."

Eagle's part of the program was long in coming. First the trio had to sit through a trying succession of unimpressive jugglers, barely adequate operatic sopranos, rheumatoid acrobats, and a mimic who imitated President Grant's fat man's strut, General Sherman's scowl, and Edwin Booth's leap to Juliet's balcony, managing to make all three look like a pudgy entertainer aping famous men. Nevertheless Miller admired how he mugged his way through his act in the face of boos, hisses, and an occasional flung glove from the audience. The man's indifference to a hostile assembly put his own crowd-fear to shame. But at last he made his exit, and after a long interval during which the stage was dark and every cough and sniffle crackled like cannonfire in the auditorium, the hard white shaft of an acetylene light impaled an empty straight chair at center stage with a pitcher and a glass on a table beside it.

Silence hung ripe while a scarecrow figure attired in black tails and a stiff shirtboard groped his way to the chair and plunked himself down. A much longer pause followed. The man sat with his bony hands on his knees (Miller noted that his cuffs came no farther down his wrists than ever) and his face slowly turning brick red. The audience began to titter.

The titters became true laughter when the man lifted the pitcher with a shaking hand and overfilled the glass, soaking the table and his own lap. But he set down the pitcher without visible agitation, brushed off his trousers, and took a drink. Took another while the commotion settled. After a short silence he began speaking in that Arkansas twang that carried like a guitar note.

"My granddaddy was the last chief of the Cherokees," he began. "He led the march when the tribe was ordered removed to the Nations by Old Hickory. Old Hickory, that's what you white folks called

President Jackson. We Cherokees had another name for him, but the sign says Ladies Welcome so I won't say what it was.

"My maw ran a trading store in the Nations. Really it belonged to my granddaddy, but in the Cherokee tribe it's the women that take care of business. Sort of like with you white folks." This brought an appreciative snicker from his listeners. "I don't know who my daddy was. He could of been the Creek boy who worked in the back room or a white circuit rider named Peachstone from Mobile, Alabama. Maw never said and she died birthing me. My granddaddy raised me to eight and then *he* died. I was on my own after that."

He drank some more water. The audience waited.

"I stole my first horse when I was ten," he went on. "It belonged to a Choctaw farmer named Billy Shut Eyes who come after me with his brothers and beat me with harnesses and turned me over half dead to a deputy U.S. marshal who took me to Little Rock and throwed me in the basement jail for three weeks until my trial come up. The jail was just a big room with two dozen men in it and a hole in the floor. Judge found me guilty of horse thieving and sent me up to the Detroit House of Corrections for eleven years. I was tall for my age, see, and there wasn't no records to prove I wasn't sixteen. Well, the ladies are still with us so I won't say what went on in Detroit. Point is they turned me loose after seven years on account of I was a good prisoner and didn't kill nobody inside.

"Meantime things had changed in the Nations. Horse stealing had got to be a big business and just about everyone had a thumb in it, including some deputy U.S. marshals. Well, with my previous experience and what I learned from them boys in Michigan I got right in there and come up real fast. We'd steal the horses in the territory and sell them in Missouri and Kansas, where the homesteaders was paying top dollar. Mostly we rustled them in bunches from corrals at night while their owners was asleep, but sometimes we had to shoot a rider off a good one. I took to that too.

"One of the fellows I was riding with, a Creek breed called Floyd Lighthorse, shot one off a strawberry roan and he turned out to be a deputy marshal. The marshal had stole the horse himself, but that didn't cut no water with the court, and we had to clear out of the Nations where they put out a shoot-on-sight order. I was still wanted there last I heard. Floyd Lighthorse, I heard he went back there year before last and got his head blowed off his shoulders resisting arrest. Anyways, I never did. I moved my business 'twixt Nebraska City and Springfield. During that time I suffered from the sin of sloth and lusted after women of arguable virtue. I dipped snuff, befogged my wits with rum, and behaved generally as a beast of the field. It was about then I met John Miller."

There followed a reasonably accurate—disconcertingly so—account of Eagle's experiences with Miller and the Missouri Militia, of his bandit career with the Stark brothers, and of the deaths of Otto Lundgren, Fick Wilson, and Lundgren's bookkeeper, Thomas Keogh, in Emporia. Someone booed when the half-breed suggested that Wilson was the only man armed among the opposition in the fight at the store, but Miller wasn't sure if the critic was denouncing the storyteller or Miller himself.

A fearful tale of gambling and biblical greed came next. The speaker paused then to fill his glass again and shake the pitcher as if determining how much water was left. He seemed to be timing himself by the frequency with which he lubricated his throat. He drank and said, "The police in Springfield arrested me in '69 for murder when a woman I knowed named Emma Woodlawn woke up dead with her throat cut one morning. Her second husband, this here old trapper, tried to claim I busted in and outraged her and then cut her to keep her tongue quiet, but he confessed finally and said he done it when he was drunk. They hung him for it sober. Apart from that I been leading a peaceable life since Kansas, trading in honest-bought horses. I'm forty-one and too old and smart for the other."

He grinned then for the first time, but Miller was seated too far back to tell if he still had his iron tooth.

"You're looking at a authentic colorful character from the Golden West," he said. "Boys, watch yourselves and stick to that straight and narrow or you'll wind up just as authentic and colorful and broke, or dead. Ladies, keep an eye on your daughters and see they marry proper or they might wind up birthing more just like me. Men, leave that cork in the bottle if you don't want to finish wearing a hemp cravat like Emma Woodlawn's husband Sam."

The advertising curtain rolled down to a spatter of applause.

In the lobby afterward, Winthrop Leland pulled on his gray cotton gloves savagely. "We now know why Eagle's book failed. If he were

not such a pathetic figure I would advise you to seek legal redress for
the calumny that you made a deal with him over the money he stole
from the bank in Emporia."

Miller said, "How do I get backstage?"

Stackable looked concerned. "The man is just jealous. There is no
sense answering him. Judging by the audience reaction, both Eagle
and his canards will be forgotten soon enough."

The gun man turned murky eyes on him and smiled. "I ain't fixing
to kill nobody my first day in town. This ain't Laramie."

After a moment, Stackable smiled too.

Miller almost bumped into a man coming out the open door of the
dressing room. He had on a tight collar that at first appeared to be
turning his face red, but on closer examination the skin had merely
been scrubbed pink, a condition common to entertainers accustomed
to applying and removing greasepaint. Miller recognized the pudgy
mimic, who looked him over swiftly in his western attire and leered.

"One frontiersman to a show, sorry. Try the Palace."

"I'm looking for Isham Eagle."

He turned his head. "Hey, injun, here's an admirer."

"Man or woman?" called out the familiar twang.

"Well, it's woman size, but it's got a moustache, so—" His cheek
brushed the Schofield's muzzle as he turned back. His eyes crossed
and he stepped aside to let the visitor past. Miller walked in and put
away the revolver without turning around. He heard the mimic's foot-
steps fading away down the passage.

"Every time we meet it's over your gun," greeted Eagle.

The half-breed was seated alone at a bench facing a long mirror on
one wall of a big room cluttered with shoes and newspapers and
discarded pieces of costume and towels smeared with greasepaint and
mascara. His tailcoat hung on a tree next to the door and he was in
his vest and shirtsleeves with the pitcher and glass from the stage in
front of him on the dressing table. As he poured, draining the pitcher,
the acrid smell of fermented juniper berries reached Miller's sensitive
nostrils.

"I thought that was water."

"I tried water in Kansas City the first night." He swallowed. "It
don't do gin's job."

Eagle hadn't turned from the mirror. His features in reflection looked far older than forty-one. The gloss was gone from his hair and his face was bloated and lumped with whiskey welts. His eyes, always muddy, lacked focus. Miller said, "You look like raw hell, Ish."

"Not by a Missouri mile. Son, I spent time there and it's worse than anything you could feature. You come to kill me for what I said out front?"

"I was to start doing a thing like that, there wouldn't be nobody left between here and the California coast."

"If you was to decide to do it I couldn't defend myself. I sold my guns and my horse for a railroad ticket and three nights' rent on this here barn. Cheap bastards at the Dime Press wouldn't even go my fare from St. Louis. 'Your book hasn't repaid the sum originally advanced, Mr. Eagle. It's a question of simple economics.' I got a tapeworm older than the editor said that to me." He emptied his glass.

"You drew a fair crowd."

"Always do the first night. Tomorrow night you could touch off a twelve-pounder out there and kill nothing bigger than a rat on a rafter. It was the same in Kansas City and St. Louis. They don't pay to hear it told straight. They want angels and devils. A goddamn Bible reading."

"You ought to of lied."

"You think I don't try? Tell it like we made up stories to stay warm when the Major said to keep a cold camp? Only they don't come out. I reckon I used up my store. You got anything needs drinking?"

Miller uncorked the steel flask he carried and filled the glass with red-tinted liquid. "It ain't gin."

"Whiskey's okay." He made a toasting gesture and poured half the contents down his throat.

"That true what you said about Emma Ashford?"

"Old Sam slipped his tether all right. Funny how a man can live with a thing for months and years without saying nothing and then just up and blow like a boiler."

"You the cause?"

"I wasn't, but he thought I was, that's the hell of it. Truth is I wasn't no good with a woman for three years after that thing at Lundgren's. I can't figure why. I was in worse in the war. But that was different."

"Emma dead. I can't see it."

Eagle grinned at his reflection, and there was the iron tooth. "You best enjoy outliving all the old girlfriends you can, John. It's the closest you'll come to a proper old age."

"Ish, that sounds mighty threatsome."

"That ain't how I meant it. Life I lived, I should be dead five years. Life you lived, you're dead now. It ain't work to get old doing."

Miller stopped up the flask. "You're some drunk."

"When you lose your place to go back to, you go to looking for it under a cork."

"Speaking of going."

For an instant Eagle's eyes came into focus on Miller's reflection in the long mirror. "Watch your friends, John. They're what's left after all your enemies are dead."

The visitor left. Three nights later, Isham Eagle hanged himself from the gas fixture in his South Side hotel room. But by then John Miller was aboard a train six hundred miles to the west and the news never reached him.

CHAPTER TWENTY-TWO

The wind that combs across the plains
mills mountains down to stones;
Sweeps dust across man's earthly gains,
and over Gun Men's bones.

Yankton, Dakota, May 1880.

All of the oaken pews in the courtroom were taken, but the court officer had granted some twenty people standing room in the rear before the doors. Behind the tall bench the judge, a Pennsylvania farmer's son with faded red hair and a broad face from which forty years away from the field had failed to remove a single freckle, rocked his chair back and forth gently and tapped the handle of his gavel occasionally for silence. He had oversensitive ears and had once ordered an attorney removed for clicking his false teeth. His name was Hunt.

The prosecuting attorney, a troubleshooter named Arrowsmith hired by the family of the deceased to assist the territorial prosecutor, was a big man as old as Judge Hunt, with a pink, clean-shaven face wallowed Pickwick-style in a high wing collar and a great shock of white hair ostensibly parted in the center but otherwise allowed to grow in whatever direction pleased it. That direction at the moment lay in front of his face as he stood leaning forward across the prosecution table with his palms flat on the glossy top.

His opposite number, James Prather, an unprepossessing man in his middle years with walrus moustaches and a large dome under a little hair, seldom looked up from his notes spread out on the defense table. On those rare occasions when he felt moved to object to something his colleague had said, he would raise his stub of pencil and do so in a conversational tone that cut across Arrowsmith's stridency like a blunt finger plucking a guitar string wound too tight. He had served two terms in Congress and was now on permanent retainer to the Badlands Stockmen's Association.

Lodged figuratively somewhere between these two widely flung types, the tawny-moustached witness sat in the box with his knees together and his hands resting on his thighs. He had on a black suit expertly tailored to his slender frame but beginning to show wear at the cuffs. His linen, however, was spotless. His expression was relaxed but alert. In this it was as normal.

"Your name is Eugene Morner and your occupation is stock detective for the Badlands Stockmen's Association?" Arrowsmith asked quietly.

Miller said, "I just got through telling that to Mr. Prather."

"The defendant will answer yes or no," directed Judge Hunt.

"Yes."

"That is not the name you are best known by, however."

"No, most know me as John Miller."

"Have you a nickname? A diminution by which you are popularly called?"

"John by them close to me. Mr. Miller by most of the rest. Sometimes just Miller, but it depends how you say it."

"Are you sometimes referred to as Killer Miller?"

Prather's pencil came up. "Objection."

"Sustained," said the judge. "Jury will disregard the question."

Arrowsmith straightened, smoothing back his hair with a palm. "What exactly does a stock detective do, Mr. Miller?"

"Regulate trespassing and rustling on land owned and controlled by members of the Stockmen's Association."

"By 'regulate,' you mean—?" The prosecutor raised eyebrows carefully penciled black.

"Well, stop it."

"Stop it how? By force?"

"When it's necessary. Mostly I just run off trespassers."

"What do you do with suspected rustlers?"

"When they let me, hold them for the law to collect."

"And when they do not?"

"Your honor, this line of questioning has nothing to do with the matter before this court." Prather seemed to be addressing the table in front of him.

The prosecutor wheeled on him. "On the contrary, Mr. Miller's admitted complicity in previous murders has everything to do with the murder he is charged with currently."

Hunt tapped his gavel handle. "Mr. Arrowsmith, the defendant has admitted to nothing. You haven't given him that chance. Your objection is overruled, Mr. Prather. I would hear this."

"I shot some men in my own defense," Miller said.

"How many have you killed—in your own defense, as you put it— since coming to Dakota?"

"Two or three. I don't rightly recollect."

Arrowsmith circled in front of the prosecution table. "I'd like to state for the record that since Mr. Miller's arrival in the territory in November 1879, six men have been found shot to death with a large-caliber rifle on lands owned and controlled by the Badlands Stockmen's Association." He seized a lever-action rifle from the long table in front of the jury box and thrust it rattling in front of Miller. "Do you recognize this weapon?"

"Yes, it's my Evans."

"By which you mean the Model 1877 .44-40 Evans repeating rifle, with a magazine capacity of twenty-six rounds?"

"Yes, it was taken from my cabin when I was arrested."

"You are aware that the bullet that was removed from Earl Weathers' heart was a .44, such as is fired by this rifle?"

"Be pretty hard not to be, the way you and Mr. Prather been yapping about it for three days now."

"Yes or no?"

"I heard some such."

Arrowsmith returned the rifle to the table. "Did you know the deceased?"

"I seen him a time or two."

"Did you in fact speak with him on at least one occasion, that being April thirtieth of this year in Clawson's Emporium in Rapid City?"

"I talked to him there. I ain't sure of the date."

"Did you not in the course of that conversation and in front of at least two witnesses threaten his life if he were found in possession of stock belonging to Lawrence Nadine, a member of the Stockmen's Association?"

"He was using a running iron to change the brand on Rocking N stock to his own Circle W."

"Liar!" A brown-faced man with straight black hair started up from his seat in the gallery. "My brother never took a thing he didn't have coming to him."

"Sit down, Mr. Weathers," ordered the judge. "I've warned you before about these tantrums. One more and I'll have you thrown out."

The court officer took a step toward the brown-faced man, who sank back into his seat, eyes glittering hate at the man in the witness box.

"Did you threaten his life?" Arrowsmith repeated.

"I don't recollect."

"Are we to assume by that that you are so accustomed to issuing death threats you cannot remember to whom you made them?"

"Everyone does that from time to time. It don't mean nothing."

"It does when they follow through on the threats." The prosecutor tossed his head, flipping snowy strands away from his eyes. "Reference has been made in these proceedings to a list of thirty names drawn up by the Stockmen's Association. Have you see this list?"

"No."

"Are you aware of its significance?"

"Just rumors."

"Did these rumors state that the small ranchers whose names appeared on that list were to be shot on sight as suspected rustlers, and that Earl Weathers was one of those names?"

"Objection. Hearsay."

"Sustained."

"I find it hard to believe that you, a stock detective, were not made privy to such a list."

"Your honor!" Prather showed agitation for the first time. He had shifted his attention from the table in front of him to Judge Hunt, who said:

"Mr. Arrowsmith, mistrials have been declared over this kind of behavior."

Arrowsmith glared at Miller a moment longer, then spun on his heel and returned to his table. "Your honor, I am through cross-examining this—man." He sat down.

"Redirect, counselor?"

Prather rose, shuffling through the papers before him. "Once again, Mr. Miller, were you playing poker in Rapid City at the time Earl Weathers was shot on property registered to Lawrence Nadine, as five witnesses have testified?"

"Association men," snapped Weathers' brother, who was immediately and roughly escorted from the courtroom by the officer at an order from the judge.

"I was," Miller replied.

"No further questions. Your honor, the defense rests."

The trial ran into the next day while each attorney presented his closing remarks—Arrowsmith's impassioned, Prather's matter-of-fact and detached—and Hunt charged the jury in a bored singsong, like a conductor calling out destinations. When the twelve men retired to deliberate, two deputy marshals removed Miller to his cell in the jail, where a visitor waited.

He stood with a soft hat in his hands in the passage while the prisoner was ushered inside and the door clanged shut between them, a small man shorter than Miller, in a dark gray suit and black cravat with a steel watch chain strung across a thickening middle. There was more gray than black in his close-cropped beard and he had a few steely hairs combed diagonally across a skull that was otherwise bare. His eyes were a curious light gray.

"Eugene, we seem destined always to meet with guards present."

"You could of come to see me at the Rocking N before this, Mr. Honey," said Miller. "Or is it still Captain?"

"I resigned my commission at the end of the war." Ben Honey glanced at the marshals. "Could we have a few moments?"

"Five minutes," said the older of the pair, a black-whiskered man Miller's age with a powder burn staining one cheek. They withdrew farther down the passage.

When they were beyond earshot Honey said, "I deemed it wise not to be seen with you before this. I am not the owner of the Four Sixes, merely its manager. The eastern interests I represent are sensitive about mixing in with the local politics. When the Association voted to engage your services, I abstained. I imagine you know most of this."

"I heard you was a member."

"Long before your name was introduced, I argued against employing a gun man. The Congress is always ready to believe the worst of the big ranchers; actions of this nature are all the excuse it requires to send in federal troops to protect the farmers and small cattlemen. We are in the minority now, governing by might alone. When statehood comes, the late settlers will elect their own representatives and hobble the industry with laws and regulations. That term "regulator" will bend back and bite the Association that coined it yet. There is no sense in hurrying things along. We need time to prepare for the new age."

"You're starting to sound like a preacher."

"I suppose that is what I am, in a way. What do you hear from your family?"

"Nothing since before I lost a brother in Gunnison County. You ain't here to talk over home." He leaned a shoulder against the cell door.

"I have a vested interest in you, Eugene. How old are you?"

The question surprised him into answering. "Thirty-eight."

"I am sixty-four. I was just your age when I led that freighting expedition to Nebraska City for George Sharon."

"I remember it."

"I had no doubt that you would." Honey paused. "You never asked why I did what I did after you killed Curly."

"My mother told me never to ask why. Anyway, you said Sharon gave her your word you'd look out for me."

"That was the sort of thing you tell a boy who believes his mother when she says it is wrong to ask why."

Miller watched Honey, framed by bars. "She knew you from before. Where? I never seen you together and I was always with her when she went to Waterloo."

"She did not tell you? No, I guess she would not. I knew her long before Waterloo. I was one of her father's clerks when he was an alderman in New York City."

"You, a clerk?"

The light eyes glinted wryly. "That view was shared by City Hall, which fired me shortly after your grandfather retired. You see, he hired me straight out of prison, where I served five years for killing a boy my own age. He saw that my penal record was lost in the system. However, it turned up again after he left and his successor was not so inclined toward mercy. Your parents and I came West on the same wagon train. You knew nothing of this?"

"Ma never was one for talking about what was past. She hated you."

"She hated the fact that she was wrong about me. She thought because I had repaid my debt to the authorities that I was not the same boy who had stabbed another to death rather than hand him my father's beer money. When she found out differently she could not forgive me her error. Is she living still?"

"I don't know. Last time I seen her she was dead as you can get and still be breathing."

"She would be kinder toward me now, I fancy. I have changed."

Miller straightened. "Well, thanks for the visit."

"It was no hardship. I have been following your career for some time. Newspapers, dime novels, that article last year in *Harper's New Monthly*. I cannot help but claim responsibility for your success. Had I not given you that horse and pointed you toward Springfield in '54 —but I am talking to suit my age. The past is graven."

The door at the end of the passage cracked open. They glimpsed the court officer's profile in conversation with the black-whiskered deputy. The door closed and both deputies started up the passage toward Miller's cell.

"The jury must be in," Honey said. "You needn't be concerned. Judge Hunt and the local law have much to be grateful for in big cattle and all of the jurors are employed in one way or another by the Badlands Stockmen's Association. Enterprise knows rewards."

Miller stood back while the door was unlocked and opened. "You won't mind if I stay to the end anyway."

"Not at all. That is every man's right."

The so-called Badlands Business of 1880 claimed one of its last victims minutes after the verdict in the John Miller trial was announced, when Earl Weathers' brother drew a Peacemaker on the ex-defendant on Miller's way out of the courthouse and was shot to

death by two deputy U.S. marshals standing nearby. Gouges made by
the stray bullets are still visible on the lobby's marble walls.

In the confusion, Weathers' intended victim ducked the reporters
waiting to interview him on the steps outside and made his way to the
marshal's office to collect his guns and other valuables. That year he
was carrying matched derringers and a .38 Colt's Lightning double-
action revolver he had bought from the widow of a sheriff's deputy
shot down by a drunk he was arresting in Omaha. The whole thing
was only eight-and-a-half inches long, about the length of the barrel
of his old Remington, and he liked that and the reliability of the
center-fire cartridges and the time gained in not having to cock the
hammer. After twenty-six years of looking he had finally found the
gun that was right for him.

The deputy marshal who had returned it to him watched him
buckle on his gun belt and load all six chambers and seat the revolver
in its holster so that the butt stuck out in front. "Court will release
the Evans in a day or so," he said. "You're heading straight out of
town now, I reckon. There's an ordinance against wearing guns inside
the limits."

"After two weeks in that stone box I don't need to be told that
twice," replied Miller on his way out.

But before going to the livery for his horse he stopped at the
Branchwater to take the dry out of his mouth. It was a big saloon and
clean, not the Belle Fleur in Gunnison but not the Antelope either, or
Jack Stonewarden's largely functional Jackrabbit in Emporia. A
wagon wheel lamp depended from the ceiling and the wall behind the
bar was plastered over with golden-brown photographs of eastern box-
ing champions. When he entered, some of the patrons recognized
him and boiled forward to shake his hand, congratulating him, but no
one patted him on the back or slapped his shoulder. He moved
around in a sort of bubble that discouraged intimacy.

A hand who had ridden in with Lawrence Nadine to watch the
trial bought him a drink and stood at the bar talking with him for a
few minutes. Miller didn't hear any of it, just the tone, that familiar
awkward attempt at common ground between cowman and gun man,
the giving up on it finally. He seemed relieved when Miller declined
his invitation to join him and some friends at a rear table, congratu-
lated him again, and left. For a bare instant Miller had considered

accepting. But since Dick Maiden had gotten shot sitting with his back to the wall, he had avoided tables in public places, preferring a standing position in command of a mirror. The Branchwater had a nice big one with a gilt frame behind the bar. He had been quoted somewhere as saying that a good mirror was the best drinking companion a gun man could hope for.

Nursing his whiskey, he studied his next move. The job with the Stockmen's Association was over; Earl Weathers' death had ended the war in a draw for the time being, and Nadine and the rest would be anxious to have Miller on his way before more trouble broke out in the aftermath of the not guilty verdict. Folks he worked for were always happy enough to greet him and eager to see him go. But work was plentiful. Big mining interests were moving into the Black Hills, and where big met small there was always a healthy demand for gunpowder and men who knew what it was for. The railroads up North were hiring men to protect their track crews from renegade Indians and displaced farmers. Law work was coming high in places like Dodge City and Tombstone, and he had a letter in his pocket from Winthrop Leland at Popular Publications, inviting him back to Chicago any time he got tired of the frontier. The letter hinted at the possibility of a lecture tour similar to Isham Eagle's, but with sounder management and improved prospects of success. Miller was sure he didn't want to do that, but he liked the idea of getting away.

He had some money coming from the Association. Maybe he'd collect it and sell the Evans and pick up Laurel DePaul, who was in Rapid City these days paying attention to miners, and they'd travel for a spell, hire a Pullman and see some country not as flat as this bartop. He'd show her St. Louis and Chicago and maybe go as far east as New York City, see the place his mother never told him about except that she once saw a man killed in the courthouse. Well, he'd just seen that, but maybe it was different in New York City. The world was full of choices.

He glimpsed movement behind him in the mirror, a man working his way up to the bar through the swirling tobacco smoke, and gripped the Colt's handle out of raw habit. Then he recognized Ben Honey's stubble-bearded countenance and relaxed. He grinned at the newcomer's reflection and started to say, "You called it." Stopped when Honey's hand came out of his coat wrapped around the handle of an ancient Paterson, reached again for the Lightning, knew even as he got the barrel free that it was going to be years too late. Worked his throat to bring the word up from under twenty-six years of lathered horses and spent powder and dead men:

WHY?

"Because you are my son," said Honey, and light flashed and turned dark.

> His pa he worked the dirt and dust
> a-strainin in the sun;
> But John he let the plow grow rust
> and practiced with his gun.